SLAVE
GIRLS

SLAVE GIRLS
EROTIC STORIES
OF SUBMISSION

EDITED BY
D. L. KING

FOREWORD BY
ROSE CARAWAY

Published in the United States by Cleis Press, Inc.,
2246 Sixth Street, Berkeley, California 94710.

Printed in the United States.
Cover design: Scott Idleman/Blink
Cover photograph: Air Rabbit/Getty Images
Text design: Frank Wiedemann

First Edition.
10 9 8 7 6 5 4 3 2 1

Trade paper ISBN: 978-1-62778-032-2
E-book ISBN: 978-1-62778-049-0

Contents

FOREWORD

What would it be like to submit? I mean, really submit? To allow yourself a moment of powerlessness? I suppose it isn't easy. You will have to find the right companion first. Or, perhaps he will find *you*.

A very special, powerful Master that can use just the right words accompanied by the most exacting touch that will make you want to surrender to him. To obey. You will take comfort in his instructions. They will always be very simple. Simple and direct. He must entice you, prove that you can trust him so that when he touches your skin, you will want nothing more than to be his cherished slave.

Every time you feel yourself submit, it is a sublime experience, and not just for you. Your Master will ask you what you like and what you don't like, what you might also be a little curious about. Your Master listens intently and makes careful note of your deepest cravings, because he knows that you are entrusting your body and mind to him. He promises with a heated glow in his eye that he will take care of you, give you everything you want. And that is precisely what he wants: when you relinquish your control to your Master's capable hands without hesitation and without fear that is your gift to *him*. He will lovingly guide you.

Your Master will worship you. He will worship your body by eliciting your desires and teasing your flesh. He will make you hunger for his touch, make you want to please him. You are a treasure in the Master's eyes. That is your gift to him, in return for his attentive care. His commands center your mind. His hands are tangible focal points for which your body begs. Your eager response is the Master's goal. His loving hands will tell you the truth about yourself, that you want him to command you, his beautiful slave.

This kind of submission, complete and confident, isn't always about the physical orgasm. He knows this. The smallest of details can evoke the most powerful, fulfilling response; the Master directs each and every sensation until it evolves, becomes a concentrated lure of pain and pleasure, pulling you closer to exquisite perfection. The Master will guide you away from resistance until your submission becomes nothing short of a religious experience.

Submitting is as much about mutual desire as it is a partnered understanding. A marriage of give and get, want and take. The Master accepts this gift as a treasure above all else.

When his commanding words and caressing breath feather across your flesh, you will know if he is the one. Your body's response will tell you.

He will teach you how the forbidden can become the bidden.

But only if you are a good girl...

Rose Caraway

INTRODUCTION

What is it about power exchange and sexual submission that just does it for me? When I ask myself that question I go a little weak in the knees, and I get that shiver through my body that makes my flesh feel a little like Jell-O. The world stops for a minute while my brain travels to the last good scene I remember. Maybe it was something I read yesterday afternoon, or maybe it was something that I did last night. I know you know the feeling; it's a Pavlovian response. Maybe you start to salivate a little, like Pavlov's dogs. Maybe it's not your mouth that starts to salivate. But it's that craving; that need. You know exactly what you need and the craving for it won't stop until it's been satisfied.

Sexual submission. My mind goes to that place. That *ooh... and then what happens?* place. You've just opened the cover to a world of handpicked stories specially written to awaken that need and/or satisfy it. Well, the stories won't satisfy it, but you know what will. Here are twenty-one stories to get you ready, to put you in just the right frame of mind; you know what I mean.

Here's a good illustration:

He pulled her wrists together so that they formed a cross and he wound his belt carefully around them, making sure to twist it both ways so that she couldn't simply wriggle free. "Like I said, I don't want you to get hurt."

These last words were whispered close to her ear. Melissa felt the first hot pulse of liquid soaking into her underwear.

He's standing right up against her back when he binds her and whispers those words to her. That's from Victoria Behn's story, "Hell-Bent for Leather." Jell-O, right?

Actually, the words, "I don't want you to get hurt," or "I just want to make sure you're safe," or "I wouldn't want you to get cold," said in the right context, can turn you into a wet mess, can't they?

How about words like these:

"I know you," he said, "you smell like earth. You taste like heaven. You need to be greased up and have things inserted into your holes. You need to be bound down. You need things done to you..."

That's from Alison Tyler's story, "Cubed." Need...things... done... Oh yeah, there's that full-body shiver.

And that's not all—not by a long shot! What else will you find in *Slave Girls?* There are stories by some of your favorite writers. Sommer Marsden's story, "Breathe," is about a woman with crippling social anxiety. Glenna finds it hard to breathe at gatherings of more than two people. There will be a reward waiting for her if she can just make it through thirty minutes of a party—a reward that will literally take her breath away.

How about a little pony play? Teresa Noelle Roberts knows just how to smooth you into that world, even if it's a completely new concept for you, just like Myra. She's normally shy and a little skittish around strangers, but Zan has the perfect way to put her at ease in "Bridle Party."

"Out of Sight" will keep you on edge and panting for more. Let me just say five words: blindfold, hotel room, strange men. This is the kind of story Rachel Kramer Bussel's known for. So hot you'll be reaching for the ice—or maybe you'll be reaching for something else.

Slave Girls is true to its name; it's all about female submission, but it's female submission served several different ways. Most of the stories have alpha-male doms good at bringing women to their knees, but there are other forms of submission. You'll find a few women submitting to women and even a ménage story with two men, one of them transsexual, playing with their submissive pet.

From the first story, "Noise," by Evan Mora, all the way to the closure you'll get from the last story by newcomer Lydia Hill, "My Master's Mark," I hope you'll find reading this book to be a very special experience; it certainly has been for me.

D. L. King
New York City

NOISE

Evan Mora

There's so much noise I can't escape it: traffic, street life, elevator music, banal conversation and false laughter. My own cynical inner monologue underscores it all; I can't even quiet that. It reaches a crescendo mid-phone call, mid-meeting; someone's rapping on the door, and I feel laughter or a scream (I can't quite decide which) pushing against my clenched-shut teeth behind my perfect, plastic smile.

It recedes little by little as the hours go by. Meetings end, the phone stops ringing and the drive home in the chilly midwinter dusk is blessedly quiet. Except for my fingers drumming against the steering wheel. Except for the mental list I'm compiling of work still undone, emails still to answer and the seemingly endless number of tasks that still need attention at home.

I should go there, but instead I call you and ask if I can see you. You say yes, and I alter my course, heading uptown to your address. The lion's-head knocker on your heavy wooden door stares knowingly as I wait. I brush my hands nervously down the sides of my skirt and straighten my jacket under his watchful eye. Then the door swings inward with an ominous groan, and my breath catches at the sight of you. Framed in the golden entryway light with your shirt unbuttoned above bespoke suit pants and a tumbler of scotch cradled absently in your palm, you bid me enter with a casual gesture, then close out the early night behind us.

You ask me what I need, the rich tenor of your voice as smoky as the scotch that even now, I know, lingers on your tongue. That you know what I need matters not. It's a part of the ritual—the naming of my desires. It has been from the beginning.

"I need..." I say, eyes fixed somewhere below your open collar, on the skin that I know will feel smooth and hot beneath my mouth. You grasp my chin in your hand, exerting enough pressure to force my gaze upward until I am caught by the impossible arctic blue of your eyes, eyes that appear at once cold and remote and yet burn like the hottest of flames. You arch an aristocratic brow at my silence and the words spill out, the words that never change, words of hunger and longing and desperate, desperate need.

In the silence that follows you weigh my words while your hand slides lower, spanning my neck. Little by little you tighten your hold, and while your gaze never leaves mine I know you miss nothing—not the flutter of my pulse against the pad of your thumb or the convulsive swallow I can't control as the pressure and my need for air mount. I don't close my eyes, even when stars threaten and your mouth covers mine with brutal intensity, stealing my reflexive gasp. I want you to see the surrender in my eyes. I want you to know that I am yours.

I sway a little when you release me, drinking in great gulps of air, oxygen flooding my body and on its heels, arousal. I feel it tingling through my extremities and then settling deep inside me, my clit pulsing to life and a flush of warmth spreading over my skin. There is nothing that drives out the world as fast as your hand around my neck, nothing that pulls me into the space I crave so quickly.

You tell me to wait for you in the study and I make my way there on unsteady legs. A fire crackles warmly in the hearth, framed by two well-worn leather wingbacks angled atop an antique Persian rug. Adjacent walls house floor-to-ceiling bookcases filled to overflowing with rare books and first-edition classics; tomes on everything from renaissance architecture to modern art; and everywhere, medical journals and texts ranging from anatomy to cardiovascular physiology. A heavy mahogany desk features prominently in front of one such wall, illuminated by the green-gold glow of the banker's lamp perched atop it. On the fireplace mantel, a black-and-white print entitled *Orchid with Devil Shadow* holds an unassuming place to one side, and yet I know it is one of your most prized possessions.

I remember standing transfixed at a gallery exhibition of some of the artist's more controversial works, images of bondage and sadomasochism, when a stranger spoke beside me: "You like these, don't you?" you said to me, and I replied politely that the artist had a brilliant eye. "Oh, come now," you chided me softly, leaning closer so that I could feel the heat of your breath against my ear, "you're so hungry I could feel you all the way across the room. Or will you tell me I'm wrong?" I looked at you then, saw the same hunger reflected in your eyes and found that I couldn't look away. "No," I said, shaking my head slightly, "you aren't wrong." Triumph flared briefly in your crystalline gaze, and then you turned back toward the exhibit, tucking my hand into your elbow as you did. "Good," you said with evident pleasure. "Very good."

I'm drawn from my reverie by your return, black medical bag

in hand. Inside are all the tools of your trade: this is how you heal me. You place the bag on the desk and withdraw several different items, laying them neatly in a row. You tell me why you have selected each item, how each will feel in turn. My body tightens with awareness and anticipation, responding to the mere promise of your touch.

You tell me to undress and I hasten to comply, eagerly shedding my dull office attire and turning to place my clothes on one of your chairs. Before I can turn back, you've captured my arms, pinning them against my sides, the hard length of your body pressing tight against the softer contours of mine.

"I'm going to hurt you tonight," you whisper softly in my ear, "and I'm going to enjoy it."

I can feel your arousal hot and hard through your trousers, pressing against my ass, and it's all I can do not to squirm and push myself back into you. You release my arms, reaching up with one hand to brush the hair away from the side of my neck, teasing the skin at the sensitive juncture of my neck and shoulder with your teeth, sending shivers racing through me. You cup my breasts, holding their weight in your palms, rolling each nipple between thumb and forefinger, gently at first and then harder, twisting each peak painfully until I do squirm, pushing my breasts into your hands, my ass into your cock, my restless hands reaching back to stroke your hard thighs. You bite down on my neck and I cry out in surprise, a sharp, high sound that I quickly contain. It's a reprimand, I know—you release me and step away, tsking as you do.

"Hands, Marietta," you say with disapproval. "Still and again: you cannot restrain yourself."

I lower my head and clasp my hands behind my back, waiting for you to bind me. You circle my wrists methodically with heavy twine, ensuring it is tight, but not overly so. In truth and as you know, being bound is my preference, but your displeasure is so real that I can't help but feel ashamed.

"I'm sorry," I whisper to the ground at my feet.

You are in front of me in an instant, hand tight around my neck, your blue eyes glittering dangerously.

"I'm sorry, *who?*" you say softly.

"Sir!" I choke out. "I'm sorry, Sir!"

But still your grip tightens. It's dizzying—the panic, the adrenaline, the inescapable animal responses that flood through me. But more, ever so much more than that is your control, your absolute and perfect control. Of me. Of this moment.

"Please, Sir..." A hoarse whisper is all I can manage. Your stare holds such intensity it's all I can do not to lower my gaze but here, at least, I succeed, holding your eyes while you search mine for the answer to some unasked question. Whatever you find, it must meet with your approval, because the pressure on my neck eases, and for a second time, I'm drawing in great lungfuls of air, light-headed and tingling with pleasure.

You pick up the crop from the selection of toys arrayed on your desk and hold it up for me to see. You tell me that a reminder is in order: of discipline and of manners. You tap my breasts lightly, repeatedly, as you speak and, already tender from your earlier ministerings, they begin to take on a pink and rosy hue, my nipples hard and straining. When the first hard strike lands I gasp at the sharp, stinging sensation.

"Say 'thank you,' girl," you say.

"Tha...thank you, Sir." I stammer. Another strike lands, this time on the other breast, and I repeat my thanks a second and then third time, and soon I've lost track of the number, a fiery heat blossoming in my chest, and from my lips, a litany of *thankyouthankyouthankyouSir...*

When you are satisfied that the lesson has been learned, you return the crop to your desk, and after a moment's contemplation move your medical bag and chosen tools to one side. You move behind me, grasping me by my bound wrists and positioning me so that I am bent forward at the waist over your heavy mahogany desk. The wood is cool and soothing against my aching breasts, though I know that this hurt is very shortly to be eclipsed.

For a moment there is only the pleasurable sensation of your hand stroking the soft skin of my ass. A surgeon's hand, strong, yet smooth and uncalloused. Precise. Then it falls with measured force, startling and yet familiar all at once. Your rhythm is steady and even, a gift to me, I know. At times you can be unpredictable, preferring to keep me on edge and guessing. But this rhythm, hard and unyielding though it is, calms me in some indefinable way. The world and all its noise fall away and my focus turns inward. Feeling. Sensation. This is all there is.

There is a pause, the movement of air behind me as you take a few steps back. Then it comes, the hard *thud* of a heavy leather flogger. My breath hisses out between my teeth, and I squeeze my eyes shut, trying not to cry out. Again and again the flogger falls, each impact more painful than the last, and a sheen of sweat breaks out on my skin as I struggle to absorb each blow. At first, it seems a doable thing—staying quiet, holding still, maintaining some measure of grace—but all too soon I'm whimpering and squirming, pride forgotten as I plead with you to stop, my tears a wet smear on the desk beneath my cheek.

You don't stop, but then, you know you don't have to. We have other words for that. If anything, begging you to stop only inflames you and your blows fall harder, with even less time for recovery.

"Don't tell me to stop, you ungrateful bitch," you say fiercely, and I feel a wave of shame flood my cheeks.

"N-no, Sir, I'm sorry, Sir," I cry miserably.

"You come to *me*, telling me how much you *want* this, how much you *need* this, and then you whimper and cry and beg me to *stop?*" You punctuate your words with unforgiving strokes, and they burn their way deep down inside me.

"You don't *want* me to stop." It's a statement, not a question, and the flogger falls with even greater intensity.

"No, Sir."

"You *want* this." Another lash. My mind starts to float.

"Yes, Sir..."

"You *need* this." Another. The pain registers differently now; I feel it, and yet it feels so good...

"And what's more"—there's a pause, the sound of the flogger being laid down—"you *like* this."

I moan as your fingers find my wetness, stroking me, teasing me, sliding in and out of me.

"Don't you?"

You're inside me again, and it feels so good I can barely think, high on the smoky seductiveness of your voice and the feel of you slowly thrusting into me. You smack my ass smartly and I cry out, jolted back to the moment, scrambling for words, telling you in a halting breathy voice I barely recognize as my own how much I like it, how much I need it—how much I need you.

With a muffled curse you withdraw your fingers and there's another pause and the sound of your zipper lowering. I breathe heavily with anticipation and then you're there, one hand on my hip, the thick head of your cock against my cunt, and then you're pushing deep inside. You give me a moment to adjust, and I close my eyes, reveling in the solid feel of you inside me. When you move, there is no gentle preamble, no tender overture of love. You fuck me hard and deep, driving out the relentless rhythm we both crave so desperately.

There is nothing that feels as right as this; the bruising strength of your grip, my tender, aching flesh, and all too soon I feel a familiar tension coiling down low in my belly.

"Please..." I moan, and another sharp smack falls on my ass.

"Please, *what?*" Your voice is a sensual growl that I feel as much as hear.

"Please, Sir..." I push my hips back toward you, a silent entreaty that makes you slam into me, your hand fisting in my hair, pushing my face hard against the desk.

"Please, *what*, Sir, you dirty whore." There is a dark, dangerous note in your voice that tells me both how aroused you are, and not to push any further. It takes me right to the edge.

"Please, Sir, can I come, Sir?" I beg.

"Do it," you grunt, releasing my hair, both hands on my hips, fucking me with a roughness that borders on violence. Your command releases me and I splinter apart, fracturing into a thousand pieces, held to the earth by your hands and your cock and the feel of you coming apart inside me.

In the aftermath, you are everything. You release me from my bonds, speaking softly, touching gently, carrying me when I'm not sure I can walk. Down the hall and up the stairs, into the warm, comforting safety of your bed. You lay me down gently, and slip in beside me: the world blissfully quiet now.

OUT OF SIGHT

Rachel Kramer Bussel

It's hard to say at first, which is more opulent—the gorgeously appointed luxury hotel room I'm standing in, or the silk blindfold waiting for me on the king-size bed. If there was a moment of doubt about my being in the right place, the five letters sewn into the black silk in elegant white italics confirm it completely: WHORE. That is what I am tonight and every night I spend with my lover, Peter. No, I'm not a whore in the traditional sense; I don't take his money, nor does he offer. Money is, ironically, beside the point between us. I'm not a whore with a heart of gold either; neither of us is rescuing the other, except from the otherwise staid lives we lead outside the confines of hotel rooms like these—or at least, staid in comparison to what happens between these magical walls.

Inside this room, I am his whore, his slut, his slave—his whatever-he-wants, truth be told. By picking up the keys he leaves for me at our prearranged times, I am agreeing to those terms, though we've never written any of this down save for the most depraved emails, the ones I most fear would be put on display should my account ever be hacked. We don't need to make my whoredom official with a collar or a contract, because it already is; anything I do from this point on will only confirm what we both already know.

Our affair didn't start in a hotel room, though, nor has today's whoring myself out begun upon stepping through the door held by a doorman who gives me the most momentary yet telling once-over. Preparing myself for today started two days ago, with a spa day booked by him and designed to leave me sleek, bare, hairless. It's part of our ritual, and I always make sure to send him a photo of my newly unfettered lower half before I put my clothes back on. Once I forgot and he made quite sure I knew that was part of the deal.

I know I said being his whore isn't about money, and it's not, exactly—it's about power. I'm more than capable of paying for my own spa appointments as well as our hotel rendezvous, and sometimes I do, but he is always the one who books them for me—for us. Because even at the spa, when I give my name, the discreet yet knowing woman checking me in already has a dossier on me; I don't know for sure exactly what he tells them besides detailing what I'm to have done to me, but I wouldn't be surprised if he managed to slip in something about me belonging to him. Of course, none of these people would ever dare risk their business's success by letting me know they know outright, but so often, actions speak far louder than words ever could. I've been to plenty of other spas where the aestheticians chat away, asking me casual questions about my job, relationship, what have you. Here the murmurings are scarce, perhaps because they already know about our arrangement but don't want to spill the beans about being in on my secret.

That's for the best, because I wouldn't have a clue how to

go about trying to explain it while my legs or buttocks are
spread open, waiting for the drizzle of hot wax, or my skin
is being scrubbed and plucked and masked into a fresher,
smoother version of itself. I can barely explain it to myself and
have given up trying with friends. "You what?" my best friend,
who's known everything about me since we were eight, practically screeched when I whispered my confession of whorish-
ness. Among my crowd, being an actual whore, the kind who
makes bank, is far more accepted than this kind of kinky affair
will ever be; they're not against kink, but they worry about
me being used. What they fail to understand is that being used
is precisely the point for me. I love being at his mercy, at his
whim, pliant and ready for anything. And in many ways, I
don't mind not sharing the details with my caring but clueless
friends, because this way no one can dilute the magic of our
encounters. They're ours and ours alone—save for the people
Peter lets into our inner circle.

When I am preparing for our dates, I am fully focused
on my task, aware that each inch of me will be thoroughly
inspected, explored, appraised. He's made me bend over a bed
and hold myself open, while he kneels before me to get an
extremely close look. I once arrived at what I expected to be a
spa but turned out to be a high-end piercing parlor. "Right this
way," the tall, lanky young man with sky-blue eyes rimmed
with black eyeliner had said, the three words an invitation and
command at once. I'd known I could have walked away—I
always can—but my pride and curiosity wouldn't let me, nor,
I must admit, would the desire to see where this man's gaze
would take me.

It was late, ten at night, an hour before the place closed. He
led me far away into a back room and shut the door. I stared at
him with what I hoped was boldness with a dash of defiance,

but he called my bluff immediately. "You don't know what you're here for, do you, Carla?"

"Does that matter?" I spit back, trying to ignore how fast my heart was pounding. It's not like they offered thousands of choices here; piercings can only cover so many body parts.

"I should think so," he said, taking a step closer, until I could feel the heat from his body across the few inches between us.

"Fine, what am I here for?" I'd almost said "in for" but somehow that sounded all wrong.

"Studs in each nipple. And I'm supposed to test your clit for sensitivity. For some women, a piercing there is too intense. Peter wants to know which type you are."

I nodded, but couldn't muster up the breath to scoff like I'd known all that. We'd discussed piercings, but always in a vague I-wonder-what-it-would-be-like kind of way. I had wondered what they would feel like in my extremely sensitive nipples, but I should have known that with Peter, musing out loud is always dangerous. He would want to push me to see whether I'd stay put or leave and await my punishment. "Did he pick out the jewelry too?"

"Yes," said the man, who stepped just that much closer, so we were touching—not pressed up against each other, but touching nonetheless. What had Peter told him to do with me? Clearly, it was more than just giving a piercing. "Take off your shirt and bra, Carla, so I can see your nipples properly. I've heard quite a bit about them." He stared deep into my eyes as he said that, and my pussy clenched. Like every time I do something new, I was well aware that I could leave, that the words he'd said were less command than dare, but that made it even hotter. With every dare I accepted, I proved to Peter, and myself, just how much I wanted him to control me, to surprise me, to usher me deep into the world of his control.

I shifted, the seam of my jeans pressing into my sex. I never used to wear jeans, only skirts and dresses, but that's something else Peter had insisted on one day. He'd made me try on a pair without panties, then explain what I'd done, pay for them, and walk around until I'd soaked them from all his commands. I was only allowed to wear them without panties, just as certain tops and dresses I was only allowed to wear without a bra, and certain skirts or stockings without panties. Those rules applied whether I was seeing Peter or not; I got the impression he liked it even better when I followed his rules on days he wasn't going to see me, when I could have gotten away with disobeying, save for my kinky conscience.

I took off my top and bra while the man watched. I didn't ask his name, and he didn't offer; instead, he took my breasts in each hand, pulled my nipples toward him, just hard enough to make me gasp. When I did, he pinched them, twisting each one until I let out another noise, one not quite so quiet. "You'll be good while I pierce you, right? No screams. I can give you a rag to muffle your noises, if you can't handle it. I've heard you can get pretty loud." The idea that Peter had told this stranger about what I was like in bed was at once infuriating and exciting.

"I'll be quiet." And I was. I thought of Peter the whole time, of how before I'd met him I never would've imagined being the type to get anything more than my ears pierced. Yet here I was not only eager to sport beautiful silver studs in each nipple, but for them to heal so he could play with them.

They did heal, and Peter did make sure he knew exactly how much more tender and sensitive my nipples were after that, and that I knew they'd remain that way from frequent use, whether that was making me suck my nipple while he shoved his fingers inside me or him simply brushing against me in public enough to make them stand at attention. But those studs were symbolic;

as long as they were in, I would always wake up thinking of him, and any other lovers I took would see them, and even if they didn't know exactly what the metal meant, I would. I'd know exactly who I belonged to—and I liked it that way.

So as I finger the sensual silk, I savor the last few moments of sight to take in the grandeur around me. There's not a mirror on the ceiling, but there's a giant one across from the bed that can only be a sign of extreme narcissism or unabashed exhibitionism and voyeurism. I strip out of my outfit—one of his favorite dresses, hot-pink silk, no bra or panties—fold the dress and place it on top of the dresser, so he's sure to see it. I resist the urge to inspect my naked body, since I don't know how much time I have before he arrives. Instead, I climb up onto the bed and carefully place the blindfold over my eyes, running my fingers over the letters like Braille so they're positioned as evenly as possible, before I tie a tight knot. I shake my head back and forth to make sure the blindfold is held in place, then lie down on my stomach, plant my cheek to the side and reach behind me for my ankles. I grab them, and then spread my knees, smiling against the sheets as I settle in to the familiar pose.

Sometimes I'm wearing the collar he's given me and kneeling at the door, in the perfect position for him to whip out his cock and shove it in my mouth. Sometimes I'm tied to the bedposts or in the bathtub or lounging on the patio. Always, I'm following his orders. Always, I'm achingly wet when he enters the room—usually alone, but occasionally with guests. I don't always get gifts, but when I do, he likes to make good use of them immediately. I know he's been traveling and is coming to the hotel after dropping off his suitcase at home. This means he's had the blindfold both custom-made and hand delivered; as much as whore pride has taken hold in some parts of the world, it's not quite so easily commodified as the more common *slut,* which I've seen emblazoned on T-shirts, paddles, necklaces, collars and, yes, blindfolds. So the blindfold is doing double duty, making sure my whoredom has been heralded to at least one hotel employee, likely many.

I'm well aware that he could have given anyone instructions to come in right now and see me like this, and that possibility makes me shiver. I have a few vibrators in my purse, just in case. I always do; I'm the kind of girl who likes to be prepared. I would love to get one out and tease myself, let off some of the tension that's been building since I walked into the room, but I don't.

I don't know how long I stay in position, waiting, before I hear the click of the door unlocking. I know that I eventually start to drool, but there's nothing I can do about it. Somehow, more than having my sex bared, more than having the word *whore* practically emblazoned on me, it's the drool that lets me know how far I've gone, how much of myself I've given to him—or whoever walks in next. I know that the longer my pussy is held open, the more ways I think of for him to fill it. I know that I'm no longer sure whether I want it to be Peter at the door or someone he's sent with his instructions. Okay, that's not exactly true; I always want him, but having him give me away like he truly owns me ups the ante of our play. I hear two male voices talking as they enter; neither is his, though I hear his name.

"I hope Peter was right about this one," one says.

"He usually knows what a girl can take," the other says.

I keep the smile on my tilted face and try to spread my legs wider in invitation. I'm grateful for the blindfold; this way I can imagine the men looking any way I want. They can see me, but not all of me. I hear the click of a camera and am embarrassed by how wet I get from the sound.

"She looks ready," I hear next. Then, in my ear: "Open

your mouth, sweetheart." I do and am immediately greeted by a round object I know immediately is a gag. "Peter told us you like to make noise, and we don't want to alert security, though you'd probably like that—having someone new to fuck to keep them from getting upset." I grunt back in tacit agreement, wondering if they're going to give me a safeword. One of them places a bell in my hand and tells me to ring it only if I want to stop the action. "We're filming this for Peter—not sure what he plans to do with it, but he will be carefully reviewing everything."

I don't grunt at this news, just quietly absorb it, not sure if I'm disappointed or not. It sounds like he won't make it, and even though he's my supreme architect of kink, I cannot fathom wanting anyone else's ministrations more than his; still, submitting to him by proxy will make a wonderful second-best scene. Part of me is relieved because no matter what these two do, at least I can pretend, if only to myself, that Peter doesn't know, deep down, just how far I'd go for him. Or if he knows, as he will once he watches the tape, I won't be in the same room when he finds out.

One of the men grabs me by the hair and hauls me up, leading me somewhere across the room. I hear the whir of the video camera, and for a second, it occurs to me that he could be live broadcasting this all over the kinky Internet. I find out I'm correct when the blindfold is slipped off my eyes: sometimes being made to see yourself and those watching you is an even bigger challenge than the lure of the dark. The camera zooms in on me and while I'm tempted to shut my eyes, I don't.

I do what I've been trained to do: raise my head proudly and stare right at the camera. I don't smile—that would be almost mocking it—but I want whoever's watching to know that I am not the kind of woman who'll submit to just anything, no matter what it looks like from their end. I'm doing this for a higher purpose, for the deepest kind of fulfillment I get from saying yes with every inch of my body, with the entirety of my soul. I'm smart enough to know my yes will never be loud enough if I shrink away from it or feel ashamed of it. I blink my carefully made-up eyes at the camera slowly, deliberately, betraying a calm I'm actually feeling—until I hear Peter's voice booming extra loud in the room.

"Hello, sweetheart. I'm sorry I couldn't be there just now, but I am there in spirit, as I'm sure you've already figured out. You know what I expect from you, and I have no doubt you will be as obedient as you've always been with me." Then he's gone, leaving my body humming with the sound of his voice, as it always is. The blindfold slips back on, leaving me disoriented, but also relieved. The men lift me up and position me so my head is hanging off the edge of the bed. A pillow is placed under my hips.

The gag is removed and in its place something very large is placed at the entrance to my lips—I know right away it's a dildo, a gigantic one, the kind whose head I'll be lucky to fit in my mouth. It's a message meant to both humiliate and tease—humiliate when I fail to fully partake of it, and tease because Peter knows that more than any other sex act, having a hard, hot cock in my mouth is my very favorite thing in the world. It's the one sex act I can get into in a moment's notice, no matter what my mood or state of mind. It sets off my senses in the most spectacular way possible, fulfilling a primal need from deep within. It's not that I want my mouth fucked by just any old object—I want it filled by a man who needs my lips and tongue and hunger more than anything else at that very moment.

But if submitting to Peter has taught me anything, it's both that I can't always get what I want, and that, ultimately, what I want is to please him. And please him I will, I promise myself, as I open wider than I think possible. Just as the object slides inside me, I feel fingers filling my pussy, and somehow, the two work in sync; the wider my mouth opens, the more of his fingers I can take. I don't think about what I look like or the fact that I don't know these men's names or the first thing about them. I know Peter trusts them, and I know that I'm close to coming. I know that this is where I'm meant to be, the way those who climb Mount Kilimanjaro or meditate know they have reached somewhere special.

I moan around the dildo and am rewarded with a hand stroking my hair—and then the door opening. He doesn't say a word, but somehow, I can feel him in the air. *My hero*, I think, even though we both know I don't submit because I *need* rescuing, but because I want it, like it, get off on feeling like a damsel in distress, although in this case, the distress is that I haven't yet come. Peter approaches and is soon fondling my ass; I'd know his hands anywhere. "Beautiful," he says, holding my cheeks wide-open, manipulating me just as surely as he's manipulated these men. Neither skips a beat, they just continuing thrusting into me while I open even wider. With Peter here, I'm free to be the whore I was born to be. "You're going to come when I put my fingers in your ass, aren't you, Carla?"

I make as much noise as I can against the toy, almost a formality, since of course I'm going to come, but were I not to answer, I imagine the fun would stop immediately. Instead, Peter teases me yet again, with a lubed-up thumb. He knows my ass, like my mouth, can take more, but he wants me to earn it. I smile around the toy invading my mouth and revel in the sensations, the four of us filling the room with the sounds of our breathing. Peter doesn't speak as he rocks his thumb into my hole, but I know what he's thinking as my climax makes its way from the place where his thumb is penetrating me upward and out. *That's my girl, that's my whore.* Behind the blindfold I see stars, and I always will as long as I'm with him.

CUBED

Alison Tyler

J ust look at that square," the cowboy said, nodding to the
man in the corner. "What's he doing in a place like this?"

"What do you mean?"

"An old guy like that. He could be a janitor. Or a shop
teacher."

I turned to gaze into the corner of the bar where the cowboy
was pointing. I don't know why I looked. I know what shop
teachers look like, and I also knew what this man looked like.
He had short silver hair and the type of jaw made for a razor
commercial, so different from the cowboy with his baby face
and his wheat-blond wave. The quiet man in the corner and I
had been trading glances all evening—I'd felt his eyes on me,
felt his interest. The cowboy must have, too, which is why he'd
tossed out the insult.

I peeked over my shoulder.

The cowboy was all that. He was Brad Pitt in *Thelma and
Louise*. He was Matt Damon in the silly horse movie. He was

what every last one of the glittery girls in the bar wanted—and he was going home with me. At least, that's what he thought. The man in the corner couldn't have been more different with his plain, blue shirt and serious expression.

"He keeps staring at you," the cowboy said with a sneer, as if I'd find the thought as repellant as he did.

I stared back. The cowboy was wrong. The other man was not a shop teacher. He was something else—a friend of your dad's from the bowling team, or a girlfriend's father—you know the type. Slow talking, no nonsense.

When the cowboy hit the head, I walked over to the corner booth. I didn't have a plan, but I also didn't have a choice. I felt magnetically pulled to this stranger's side.

"You like the pretty boys?"

I shrugged.

"He's going to be all done in five minutes, and you know it. Preening peacock in his pristine hat. He's going to want you to adore him, when he doesn't deserve your attention. Not for a fucking second."

I looked at the crisp shirt, the old-fashioned watch, the scotch with ice.

Shop teacher? I didn't think so.

"You don't even like him. You're too smart for a sleaze like that. You just know the other tarts in here want him. And that's making you feel special."

"What are you? A psychiatrist?"

He laughed. "What you need is a spanking."

"Oh, you think so?" I asked in my best flippant tone. The cowboy thought I needed a margarita and a massage, after a good long soak in his hot tub under the stars. He'd made noises about kissing every inch of my body, about treating me like a princess, pampering me with his hands and his mouth. I hadn't confessed that a soft touch did nothing but make me squirm.

"You need to be put over my knee and have that little dress lifted up to your waist. You need your ass turned as red as the slut outfit your wearing."

The cowboy was back from the john, but I didn't move. I couldn't. What type of power did this man have over me?

"And then what?" I asked, feeling my heart pounding in every part of my body. Even my fingertips throbbed.

"Come closer."

I took a step.

"Turn around."

"Why?"

"Face your pretty boy."

"Why should I do what you say?"

Most girls would have gone with the good-looking cowboy. I knew that. But I had the shop teacher right there pulling me toward him, digging into his drink for an ice cube and telling me once more to turn around. But this time, there was a chill in his tone.

Would you believe that I obeyed? I turned around, and I felt his hand slip up the back of my dress, felt his cold fingertips— oh, fuck—place that chunk of frozen water right at the split of my cheeks. My face couldn't have turned redder. The cowboy looked confused. What was I doing out of his range? Where was his lasso? What he didn't realize was that I was the type of filly who needed to be branded.

"I ought to put you over the table, lift up your skirt and take down your panties. Spread you wide open and show off your holes. Pick a hole, I'd tell the gentlemen. And you know there'd be a line. And you know your pretty peacock would melt faster than a Popsicle on a hot summer day...his pecker going soft at the thought of having to perform under pressure."

I didn't move until the man said, "Tell him to go on without you, to choose another little heifer."

I turned back. "Why would I do that?"

"Because you want everything I just said."

"You think so?"

He laughed again, darker this time. "You need more than that, don't you? You need me to tell you everything."

I nodded, and the shop teacher reached out a hand and pulled me to him. He sat me so I was perched right on his knee, and he handed me his drink. "Take a sip." I took a sip. He pressed his mouth close to my ear and said, "You want me to tell you that after I spank you, I'm going to take you to my bedroom and cuff you down. And then, when you're good and tight, I'm going to crop you—twelve times—six this way, six that."

I shivered. He was pressing my buttons. Hard. I could feel his knee digging against my clit. I wondered if I could come while he talked to me.

"Only when you've been properly punished am I going to give you the rest."

"What's the rest?" I begged.

"I'm going to ice up your asshole and fuck you there. And by that time, doll baby, you're going to be begging me to split you wide open. You're going to be dying for it."

I didn't get up right away. I wanted to rock myself against him until I came. I wanted him to describe all the other things I fantasize about late at night. He'd hit on so many visions in two minutes. What else did he know about me?

"Look at your pretty boy," the man said again. "You know his asshole smells like Windex and tastes like salt. You know his dick is long, and thin and pink. What would you do with him? Why would you give him a second of your precious time?"

He bit my neck.

"I know you," he said, "you smell like earth. You taste like heaven. You need to be greased up and have things inserted into your holes. You need to be bound down. You need things done to you. Things he'd never even think of. Go tell him he lost," the shop teacher said, "then meet me in the parking lot."

I went to the cowboy.

"I thought you were leaving with the idiot shop teacher," he said, pleased that I was at his side once more.

"I am," I said, making the choice for real right then.

When we got to his home, he put me over his lap and spanked me. Hand spanked me until I was wet like melted butter. Was that going to be it? Some men don't live up to their promise. They get you over their lap—and that's the end of the ballgame. My last spanking had come from a beau who referred to my hindquarters as my "fanny." "You need a bright red fanny," he'd say. I didn't like the term—but I liked the spanking. Yet that's as far as he could go. No belts. No paddles. Just his hand. And then his cock.

Was this man up for me? Would he be a promise keeper?

Thank god, he was. He took me to the bedroom and told me to lie facedown on the bed. My ass was hot and red. My pussy was so wet and ready that if he had changed the plan, I wouldn't have complained. But one look in his eyes let me know that he was going to remain true to his word.

"Girls often need to be tied for this part," he said, and I liked that. I wasn't jealous at all at the implication that he treated women like this on a regular basis. I'm a fucking liar. I was extremely jealous, which made no sense. Because this was the first time I'd met him. But I will confess that I liked that he had the experience. I liked that he brought knowledge to the equation—as well as cuffs.

If the cowboy had tied me down, he would have used scarves made of silk. There would have been something playful and pretty about his bondage gear, something to make you think that he wasn't serious. The shop teacher didn't need to pretend. We both knew just how serious he was. The cuffs, well, you can guess. They were regulation, stainless steel. He didn't even bother to show me the key.

I wondered if he'd play the way they instruct you to play in all the manuals. Was he going to ask me for my safeword? Would I be able to come up with one if he did? He bound my legs apart as well, tying my ankles to the posts of his bed with leather straps. The man was prepared, I had to give him that, a regular boy scout. Or maybe a scout leader.

"You know what's coming next," the man said, and I nodded. I knew. He climbed onto the bed with me for a moment. He pressed his mouth to my ear. I felt a shiver flicker through me. There is nothing in the world like the moment before the pain starts. This is the time you tell yourself you don't need it. This is the time you make up save-yourself, fantasy, fairy-tale stories in which you go home happily with the...

"Peacock," the shop teacher said.

"Excuse me?" I was in that space, that head space that is almost like tangible white noise. A hot, sweet rustling filled my brain.

"If you need me to stop, you say, 'Peacock.'"

God, he was fucking with me. We both knew I wouldn't be able to say that word. Because that would be like an admission, like a failure, a wish that I'd gone with the cowboy. A blush hit my cheeks as hard as if he'd slapped me. He was giving me shit for having talked to his rival for so long.

The pain came next. Startling. Crystalline. Perfect.

He used a whippet-thin cane to crisscross my cheeks with

twelve blows. Not all at once, mind you. Not on your life. He let the first blow land, let me feel the pain, let me deny that I needed this, and then he struck the second blow. I was ready for the margarita and the massage. I was desperate to be free. I was on the verge of crying peacock when he was on the mattress once more, spreading my cheeks open wide, pressing his thumb against my asshole and then thrusting it inside of me, so that my body contracted on his digit, so that I could imagine just what the pleasure would feel like when he fucked me there.

Oh, he was good. You take the pain, you get the reward. That was the equation. I could accept this. But at two, two out of twelve, we had a long way to go.

"Look at my girl," he said, gripping the back of my heavy hair and turning my head so that I was facing the mirror over his dresser. "Look at how hungry she is."

I didn't want to. Seeing myself like that was like being undone, as if he'd pulled all the laces free and let loose the real me. The cowboy hadn't understood. Few men did. When you want what I want, you need to find a kindred spirit, you need someone who is unafraid. So many men are scared of me. Too many.

"You going to say it?" the man said.

I shook my head. We were at that stage. The place where I accepted a dare, his dare. I wouldn't renege. I wouldn't go back. I wouldn't let him down, because to let him down would mean to let myself down. But that's not saying that I didn't envision the cowboy, with some pert blonde, all tangled up together on a bearskin rug in front of a fire. Some people must get off on clichéd scenarios like that. Some lovers must reach their highest peaks with soft warm kisses and slow caresses and...

"Tell me you want more."

Not me.

"I want more."

He hit me with the next four blows in rapid succession. One this way. One that way. One this way. One that way. I was humming on the endorphins. But that didn't mean I couldn't see what it would be like to give up. Not to say the word—oh, no—not to say the safeword. But to give up the resistance. To let myself fall into the pit of submission. And it is a pit. Dark, velvety, slippery walled. Giving in is sublime, but it takes a lot to get there.

Years, sometimes. A whole lifetime, occasionally. Or eight blows.

Because that's what I needed. Two more. One crisscrossed over the next, and I was done fighting. I crested on the rest. The last four strokes took me to that higher plane, where sparkling silver stars bloom behind my eyelids and the pain is no longer pain and pleasure is just an eight-letter word for being alive.

"You know why I had to do that?" the man asked, as I heard him undo his buckle.

I looked at him. There were tears streaming down my face, and I had no voice.

"Because you made me wait."

I understood what he meant. I'd toyed with and teased him at the bar. I'd felt him watching me, and I ignored the call.

"That's okay, baby," he said, reaching for the ice. "Waiting makes the prize more valuable."

I couldn't stop what was going to happen next. I was bound in place, nowhere to go, no way to run. But the chill was somehow more startling than the caning had been. Inwardly, I curled up, even if my body couldn't move. He iced me just as he had in the bar, but more seriously now, running the cube all around my asshole. I groaned and buried my face in the mattress. The man laughed. That sound chilled me even more.

His hands parted the cheeks to my ass and then he was pressing the head of his cock to my hole. He could have thrust in all at once. But he didn't. He went slow, so slow, so that I was the one to arch my hips as much as the bindings would allow. Now, was the moment. His cock against my hole. Stretching me. Opening me. Making me beg.

I was the one to back down on him, making him laugh louder. I wanted this. We both knew that.

He roughed up my hair. "Good girl," he said. And then he grabbed my hips and began the ride for real. Being filled like that flipped on a switch inside of me. I felt my pussy responding, felt the juices sweet on my thighs. He made sure to run one hand under my body and stroke my clit every few strokes, so that I was sandwiched in the sensations of being filled and being touched, and when I came, he came with me.

There I was. Bound to the bed of a stranger. Hurt and calmed. Fucked with and resolved. But most of all, I was done.

He undid the bindings on my ankles, set me free from the cuffs and then wrapped me up in his white sheet. He handed me a glass of water and I took such a big sip that I spilled half of it down my chest. The chill soothed me. His embrace warmed me.

"You're beautiful," he said, and I felt it. Then, "Thank you," and I felt that, too. I didn't want to put my dress back on. I didn't want to leave. He seemed to understand. He went to his dresser and pulled out one of his T-shirts, tossed the soft cotton to me and watched as I slid it on.

"What do you do?" I asked, as I pulled the shirt over my head.

"I'm a teacher," he said, and I couldn't help but crack a smile. Shop. Was the cowboy right after all? But then he gave me a sideways grin and said: "Math."

I'd never been much good at cubing before.

But the peacock was wrong. My new man was far from square.

SERVING MR. BALDWIN

Veronica Wilde

So you're Natalie."

The executive's heavy-lidded eyes landed on my black heels and slowly rose, studying my legs, my black pencil skirt and white blouse, and then my long brown hair. His eyes descended to my breasts and stayed there. I tried to stay composed. No man had ever studied my boobs so blatantly before, certainly not in the workplace.

What did you expect? a voice in my head asked. *You did answer an ad to be an exotic secretary!*

The blinds in the office were pulled, but a faint glow from the setting sun seeped through. Outside the corporate building, cars were leaving the employee parking lot. It was after five o'clock, time for everyone to go home. No doubt that's why Mr. Baldwin had scheduled the interview now—so his real secretary wouldn't see me.

"You have secretarial experience?" he asked in his deep, cultured voice.

"Yes, I've worked as the assistant to a vice president of an office supply company for three years," I replied. "Well—I did until I was laid off last month."

"And you dressed properly," he mused, studying my simple blouse and skirt again. "Every other girl I've interview has shown up dressed like a cocktail waitress."

A jealousy rose up in me, thinking of those other girls hoping to be Mr. Baldwin's toy.

"Come here." He gestured for me to come around the vast mahogany desk. I stood in front of him, heart knocking. This close, I could smell his expensive cologne and see that his tie was silk, his suit impeccably cut. He was the picture of the cool and powerful executive, with dark hair going gray and a few lines around those wise, dark eyes.

"Unbutton your blouse," he told me.

I complied with shaking fingers. My blouse hung open, my breasts showcased in blue lace.

"Lift up your bra."

Self-consciousness flooded my face, followed by a swift bolt of arousal as I held up the bra underwire, letting my tits bounce free.

As if considering apples at a supermarket, Mr. Baldwin cupped and felt my bare breasts. Oh god. Was this really how this job was going to go? On the phone, he had told me he wanted a submissive exotic secretary who was comfortable with sexual play. I had been too timid to ask exactly how far the "sexual play" would extend.

He released my breasts and said, "Turn around." When I did, he said a bit impatiently, "Pull up your skirt and bend over."

I bent over, feeling as if I was thrusting my bottom in his face. He smoothly pulled my panties down to my knees and cupped my asscheeks much like he had my breasts. Then he ran his fingers over my inflamed pussy so lightly that my clit throbbed for more. I spread my legs a bit, hoping he would finger me.

Instead his hand withdrew. "Get dressed," he said. "You're hired. Salary is as we discussed. You'll report here Tuesdays and Thursdays, from five-thirty p.m. to seven-thirty p.m. And this is important—always wear a skirt and blouse and heels. That is the only acceptable outfit."

I tugged down my skirt. "Thank you."

"I'll see you Thursday at five-thirty." He gave me a polite smile and turned back to his desk, dismissing me.

A dozen questions flooded my mind as I walked out—what would be expected of me? How much sex would be involved? Would I be doing actual secretarial work, and would he be the only one who saw me? But I knew it wasn't my place to ask those questions; for this job, accepting Mr. Baldwin as my boss meant accepting his complete authority.

Which was just what I had always wanted.

My first evening on the job was dull. I sat at the large mahogany desk his normal secretary sat at during the daytime, and sorted a pile of filing. At my old office, we had tried to keep all of our documentation digital, to be more eco-conscious. But Mr. Baldwin's outer office was full of filing cabinets with invoices in them and he wanted them sorted by date, then amount. Mindless work, and I wondered why he would pay such an inflated wage for an exotic secretary to do it when his real assistant could easily have handled it.

Surely he'll call me into his office at any moment, I reasoned. But he didn't. I worked my two-hour shift without Mr. Baldwin laying one executive finger on me. And went home with a wet, swollen pussy aching to be used.

All weekend I wondered if I had done something wrong. Had

I not been subservient enough? "You'll be doing exactly what I tell you," he'd said on our initial call. "So if you have problems taking orders and obeying your boss's every command, this is not the job for you."

The following Tuesday I showed up in a clingy blue sweater, pencil skirt and spike heels. When he saw me, he frowned.

"I gave you clear instructions on the dress code," he said. "You are to wear a blouse, not a sweater."

"I..." I hadn't really thought it mattered that much, a blouse or a sweater. The cashmere showed off my breasts nicely, which I wanted him to appreciate.

He sighed heavily, walked toward me and pulled the sweater right over my head. I gasped as he unhooked my bra and pulled it down, backing me against the desk.

"You are to do as I say," he said, fondling my breasts. "I made it very clear how I wanted you to dress, and now you've already disobeyed me on the second day. If you always have this much trouble following orders, this isn't going to work out."

"I'm sorry. I won't have any more trouble."

He lightly tugged on each nipple, making me bite my lip. I tried not to show how badly I wanted him to keep going. He smelled fantastic, and being topless as a tall, older man in a suit loomed over me was activating every submissive fantasy I had.

"Look at me."

I looked up into those heavy-lidded dark eyes.

"I need someone I can depend on," he said, pinching my nipples. "Not a little office slut who wiggles around trying to entice me. Understood?" I nodded and he sighed. "Very well, then. Bend over."

My face went hot. Oh god. Was this really going where I wanted it to? I turned around and bent over the desk, my breasts brushing the cool mahogany. He matter-of-factly pulled up my skirt and tugged my panties down my thighs. I was now naked for all intents and purposes in a corporate office while a stern businessman loomed behind me, and the thought of what might happen next was soaking my cunt.

The first smack landed on my left cheek, making me jump. I'd played with myself so many times, dreaming of being spanked, and now the reality was here. I felt shaky, vulnerable and wildly aroused. His hand landed on the other cheek. I jumped again—I couldn't help it.

"Be still," he commanded. "Take your spanking like a good girl."

He spanked me eight more times. Of their own accord, my spiked heels spread farther apart, inviting him to look at my pussy. I was leaning farther over the desk, my stiff nipples brushing the cool surface, and panting. If only he would take out his hard cock and fuck me with it, gripping my neck.

Instead he stepped back and said, "Very well. Get to work. There's more filing for you to do." He sounded bored.

I straightened, dazed and shaky. When I reached for my bra, he slapped my hand away. "No," he said, suddenly stern. "You're not wearing that today."

So I had to work topless for the rest of my shift, my nipples painfully stiff in the office air-conditioned chill. Twice he came out of his office and checked my filing, idly playing with my breasts when he did so. But he made no move toward satisfying me, and I wondered if he ever would.

I was still looking for a full-time job and interviewing for other office support positions. I wondered dreamily if Mr. Baldwin would ever replace his daytime secretary with me. The idea of spending eight hours a day with him—keeping his calendar, scheduling his meetings, booking his travel and being called into the office on occasion to be stripped and spanked—was heaven.

On my next shift, Mr. Baldwin told me he could see that I was too intelligent to waste on filing, and he wanted to train me for more complex work. He had me sit on his lap behind his desk as he went through the company website with me and explained what the business did. "I have a project I think you'll be perfect for," he said. "You have PowerPoint skills, right?"

He slipped his fingers under my panties and stroked my clit as he explained the kind of presentation he wanted me to put together. I tried to concentrate on his words, since I knew this project would be important in my keeping this job. But now that he was finally playing with my pussy, I wanted to just lie back against his chest, close my eyes and succumb to the red-hot sensations spreading through me.

"So what do you think?" he asked. "Could you put something like that together?"

"Absolutely," I murmured. *If you can slip your fingers inside me and finger-fuck me until I gush all over your expensive suit,* I wanted to say.

"Good girl." He patted my pussy, withdrew his hand and helped me stand up. I smiled and tried not to show my frustration. Exactly what would it take to enjoy an orgasm around here? He had to need release too—right? I couldn't bear to think that he simply wanted a girl to feel up and look at—that he had no intention of truly fucking and debasing me the way I needed. I'd finally found a man who I was sure could be the Master I'd always wanted. But if he didn't fuck me soon, I was going to scream.

Of course it was obvious what I needed to do. The spanking I'd gotten for wearing my blue sweater had taught me that. But the evening I planned my next punishment held a surprise for me as well.

I was a little nervous as I walked into the office that night. I didn't know how Mr. Baldwin was going to react to such flagrant disobedience. What if he just sent me home? What if he—oh god—fired me? No, he couldn't, I thought. Not when he enjoyed punishing me so much.

He walked into the secretarial area and stopped dead. I summoned a confident expression as I stood before him in my regulation blouse, black miniskirt—and very nonregulation high black boots.

Spank me, I dared him silently. *Strip off my top and bra and pinch my nipples. Make me crawl naked through the office on all fours and suck your cock. Just do something.*

Our gazes locked. Then a blond man surfaced from Mr. Baldwin's office. He too was dressed in a suit and tie, though he was a few years younger than my boss.

"Oh!" he said. "I thought your secretary left."

"She did. I have another one who comes at night."

The stranger eyed my boots and skirt. From his dirty leer, I could tell he liked my outfit, even if Mr. Baldwin's face had been transformed with a steely displeasure.

"I'm glad you're here," Mr. Baldwin said in a clipped tone. "I need you to go to the café on the corner and bring us coffee."

They gave me the order and I left. My heart was heavy with disappointment. Nothing was going to happen this evening, not with the visitor there. I actually considered quitting when I returned with the two coffees. Maybe I was earning good money, but was the sexual frustration worth it? I'd hoped for a truly dominant man to master me, boss me around and use me sexually. Instead I seemed to be just an office pet, good for ogling and fondling and that was about it.

I knocked on his office door, deposited the coffees on his desk and returned to the outer secretarial area. Yet I'd barely sat down when the door swung open.

"Natalie." Mr. Baldwin had never sounded so stern. "We gave you the exact order. How hard is it to order two coffees correctly?"

"Were they wrong? I handed the barista your order—"

"Oh, so it's the barista's fault. Not only did you get our order wrong, but you can't take responsibility for it."

"I—I'm sorry," I stammered.

"Get in here and apologize to Mr. Crowley."

I walked into his office with my knees shaking in my boots. I felt like an idiot. "I'm sorry I got your order wrong," I said meekly to the blond man. He smirked.

"Bend over," Mr. Baldwin said.

I paused. He couldn't really spank me in front of someone else, could he? This whole arrangement we had was a secret. No one at his company knew about it. He locked the door to his office suite and closed the blinds in case anyone was working late. There was no way he could spank or strip me in front of another executive.

But his dark eyes were serious. I bent over the desk and pulled up my skirt, showing them my panties. My heart was thudding.

Mr. Baldwin tugged my panties down. I tried not to show how excited I was. I loved showing my ass off to this impudent stranger who was drinking in every detail of my body. But then Mr. Baldwin dropped into his leather swivel chair and did something I didn't expect.

"Give her twenty," he said to Mr. Crowley. "Not too hard, but don't go easy on her either."

My face flooded with embarrassment. Being spanked by my

boss was one thing. Being handed off to a stranger was another. Even worse, Mr. Crowley would clearly take every liberty he could with this spanking.

"My pleasure," he said under his breath. He stepped up behind me and softly commanded, "Spread."

It was the dirtiest word anyone had ever said to me. I spread my boots as far as my tangled panties would allow, knowing this gave him an excellent view of my bare pussy. But his hand landed on my upturned bottom a moment later and he went through the spanking quickly—the first ten blows at least.

Then he stopped. "I want to spank the rest of her."

The rest of me? What did that mean? I looked in alarm to Mr. Baldwin, whose lips twitched in a smile. But he merely shrugged and said, "Do as you will with her."

To my horror and excitement, Mr. Crowley told me to straighten. Then he stripped me so efficiently I knew this wasn't his first time undressing a submissive. Off came my blouse, then my bra, then my skirt and panties, his leering eyes drinking in every new inch of exposed skin. Finally I was naked, except for my boots—truly naked for the first time in this office.

"Lift your arms over your head."

I obeyed, keeping my eyes on the ground, and hoped it wasn't obvious how wet my pussy was.

Mr. Crowley softly smacked my left breast, making it jiggle. He did the same to the right, then the left again, then the right, as both men watched my tits bounce and sway.

"Six more," he said in a taunting voice. "And I know just where you need to be spanked." He looked between my legs and I jumped back.

"Please," I blurted. I'd never had my pussy spanked. I didn't even know men liked that. And my clit was so swollen and sensitive right now—I couldn't bear to have it spanked.

"Natalie," Mr. Baldwin barked. "What kind of rebellion is this? You'll take your spanking like the obedient secretary you are!"

He pulled me onto his lap. I was too stunned to move as he hooked his feet around my boots and forced my legs open. Mr. Crowley stared at my gleaming wet pussy with a dirty grin. I knew he could see my hard little clit poking out of its hood, begging for the softness of a tongue or the gentle touch of a finger. Instead it was going to be spanked.

His hand landed between my legs. I jumped as his fingers connected with my sensitive flesh. It didn't hurt, but it was a powerful sensation unlike any other I'd ever felt.

He spanked my cunt a second time. Oh god. Every touch made my body cry out for more contact. This was worse than teasing; it was torture. I arched my back, unable to stop myself, and spread my legs wider. Mr. Baldwin murmured in an amused, loving voice, "You little slut."

Mr. Crowley spanked me a third time. Three more to go. When the fourth slap came down, I cried out in raw need. I grabbed Mr. Baldwin's tie for something to hold on to, spreading my thighs as wide as I could. "My hand's soaking wet," Mr. Crowley said. I couldn't stop myself; as he gave me the final two spanks, I shamelessly pushed myself against his fingers, hoping he would leave them there and make me come. Instead he stepped back.

"Please," I begged helplessly.

Mr. Baldwin reached up and tweaked my painfully hard nipples. "Please what?"

"Please make me come."

Both men laughed. I was pushed off Mr. Baldwin's lap and onto my knees a moment later as they both unzipped their pants. Suddenly there were two hard cocks in my face. "Suck us," Mr.

Baldwin told me coolly, "and do a good job if you want to keep working here."

I opened my mouth and sucked in his prick. That familiar masculine taste of hot, salty skin and a drop of sweet precum filled my tongue. My boss's cock was in my mouth at last and I was determined to impress him. I sucked and licked his head, wanting desperately to please him. Mr. Crowley laughed. "That is one eager little slut," he said. "She's so horny she'd probably suck off anyone right now."

Yet suddenly Mr. Baldwin pulled his cock from my lips. I looked up at him in betrayal as Mr. Crowley replaced him, his stubbier cock filling my mouth. What had I done wrong? But I gave Mr. Crowley the best blow job I could, hoping he would come quickly so I could return to Mr. Baldwin.

Then Mr. Crowley pulled out and ejaculated all over my face, groaning as he decorated my lips and cheeks with white cum.

"Stand up," Mr. Baldwin ordered.

I tried but was too disoriented and shaky to keep my balance in my boots. They laughed and lifted me onto the big mahogany desk. I spread my legs in open invitation. Never had I felt so dirty or so aroused—showing my pussy to two men, with a stranger's cum on my face.

Mr. Baldwin's thick cock pushed into me. Finally. My boss was fucking me with vigor and abandon, thrusting in and out of me with primal grunts. His tie swung over my face as he pumped into me, driving me into the most dangerous kind of bliss—the kind where I wanted to submit to him utterly and always, as long as it involved this kind of ferocious union. He really was the Master I'd been looking for; I knew that now by the way he commanded my pussy so completely. I groaned and succumbed to the euphoria filling me, my cunt throbbing around him. He shuddered and pulled out, milking his cock to come all over my tits.

Finally he straightened and ran a hand across his reddened face with an embarrassed smile. Mr. Baldwin didn't lose his cool executive air too often. "Not bad," he said in a nonchalant voice. "Get dressed and clean yourself up. And remember, Natalie—wear the heels your next shift. That's an order."

"Yes, Mr. Baldwin."

I walked out with a smile. I would be wearing heels the next time. Maybe I would be naked except for the heels; maybe he would share me with another friend, or make me beg for his cock in some newly naughty way. Whatever happened, I couldn't be more ready or willing.

PRESS MY BUTTONS

Nina Fairweather

P osters announced a sale on vitamins and discounted toiletry
prices. Twin doors slid open as I approached. Dozens of
fluorescent tubes suggested quantity but not necessarily quality.
Tabloid magazines insisted movie stars were pregnant with
alien babies. It could have been a corner drugstore anywhere.

I dug a shopping list from my backpack and walked directly
to the vitamin aisle to find a straight-girl cliché between me and
the brand I liked. Blonde, in a skirt and sweater, she reached for
a bottle from the shelf and I noticed her nails. They were long
and painted the exact red of her lipstick. Why did I even bother
to look?

"Are you a doctor?" she asked. "Would you mind giving
me a little advice?" She must have noticed that the company
name on my name badge contained the word *health*. Perhaps
she wasn't a clueless dye-job.

"No, ma'am," I told her, "I'm a nurse and I drive a desk most
days, but I'll do my best."

We talked and I noticed that she seemed very proud,

dignified. She held her chin high. Her gaze was piercing. She swept it over my body more than once before it returned to hold my own gaze. I found my field of vision lowered instinctively.

I grinned when she slid behind me in the checkout line. So did she, warmly enough that I questioned my earlier conclusions. Perhaps she could be a little fun after all. In fact, with those boots on...

She had me swooning enough that my voice seemed to act on its own, blurting out, "May I buy you lunch?" as the clerk rang up the last of my items. The woman tallying my items blushed and carefully counted out my change. I barely noticed. The tall blonde behind me in line had my full attention.

Fifteen minutes later we strolled into one of my favorite diners. She introduced herself as Lynn. She ordered noodles with basil and chicken. I requested the same. We prepared to share an order of spring rolls.

"I like your political buttons," she commented.

I grinned. "Did you read them all?" She shook her head so I held my backpack on my lap for display.

"I like DIP ME IN HONEY AND THROW ME TO THE LESBIANS and ORGASM DONOR but I think I like the ones near the bottom best," she said, after I returned my bag to the ground under our table. The lower portion of my bag was reserved for kinky buttons. One depicted handcuffs. Another read SLAVE with a chain motif border. Still another read, EVERY TOP NEEDS A BOTTOM with deliberate upper- and lowercase letters.

I grinned again. "You're familiar with them?"

She cocked her head slightly to one side and scanned my eyes. I silently begged her to trust me.

"Yes," she finally answered. Then she took a drink of water. I wondered if she talked to many people about BDSM. Was I the first? Was she merely cautious?

"Are you dominant, then?" My heart fluttered. I wanted her to say yes. I wanted her to tell me that she didn't have a submissive of her own.

Lynn smirked. Then a waitress placed spring rolls on our table. "Thank you" rolled out of my mouth when what I really wanted to say was, "Go away!" or "Do you think she wants to tie me up and tease me until I beg for release? I hope so!"

Our fingers tore into the spring rolls. When Lynn finished she folded her napkin and placed it on the table. I nearly panicked. Was she leaving? Was I too candid?

She leaned forward, waited a moment and whispered, "I won't say more here, but I'd like to talk about it somewhere more private. Is there a quiet park nearby?"

I thought for a moment. "One, but we won't find much privacy there," I replied. "My apartment building has a garden patio on the roof. It's quiet, if a little windy, and only a few blocks away." I forced myself to stop talking. Was that too forward?

Our noodles arrived. Lynn was quiet until after three bites. "I think that will do." I nodded and changed the subject in an effort to rid us of anticipatory silence. I discovered she had an interest in local politics. I gently prodded her with what I hoped were polite political questions.

She paid the check. I offered to help, but she wouldn't hear of it. I thought briefly of kneeling beside her and begging but settled for pulling on my coat, grabbing my backpack, and following her to the door.

As expected, Lynn and I had the roof of my apartment building to ourselves. We both remained quiet for several minutes after sitting side by side in lawn chairs. I enjoyed the contrast in sound and smell thirty floors above car exhaust and constant chatter.

Lynn's voice pulled my attention from the world around us.

I blinked. "Did you say something?"

"I answered your question from earlier today."

My mouth became a desert. "And what was the answer? I'm sorry, I missed it." However, I didn't really need to hear that word fall from her lips. I knew.

I could tell by the way she leaned back in the lawn chair, her hands folded together, her interlacing digits forming an intricate pattern of soft fingers and sharp, red nails. I knew by the shark's grin that painted her face and the jaguar's sparkle in her eye.

The sky raged behind her. Clouds became odd fountains, spilling shapes into the cerulean sky. Yet none of it matched her intensity even though she merely sat still in a chair. I tried to imagine her standing over me holding a crop, flogger, or worse, a look of disappointment. I squirmed.

"It's a wonderful view," she said, looking directly at me.

My cheeks warmed despite the breeze. I looked off in the distance toward the water of the bay. "Yes, it really is." I tried to pull attention from myself. "When the sun sets the sky turns purple and, if the weather is clear enough, the mountains are silhouettes." She rose from her chair, and soon I heard the soft click of her heels behind me. I thought of turning around but decided against it. Then I felt her hand brush my hair away from my neck.

Her lips felt like embers in the cool air so high above the city streets. Their heat against the tender back of my neck left me shivering. She seemed to notice. Her arms wrapped around me. I managed to whisper, "Thank you."

Her breath was warm on my ear, but her voice was icy. "I didn't like you prying about my kink preferences in public," she stated.

I swallowed. "I'm sorry. I..." I began, but she cut me off. Her voice held intensity yet hardly rose above a whisper.

"No, you're not sorry yet." She paused. "Do you live alone?" Then I saw her waver. Before I could answer she spoke again. "No, wait. You don't have to answer that. We just met and you should be careful.

"But we can still have fun." Her head tilted to one side. "Do you know what a safe call is?" I nodded. I didn't give her enough credit. She knew far more than I guessed. "Good." She pulled a phone from her jacket.

"Thank you," I said, "But…" I held up one finger and then crossed the rooftop. I retrieved my backpack and returned to the striking blonde.

Her eyebrows were raised. "You better have a damn good reason for that nonchalant 'Just a minute' little finger of yours." I smirked and retrieved a phone from my backpack. Lynn nodded.

I made arrangements from the opposite side of the roof and set an alarm on my phone. I found Lynn staring west when I looked back at her. She turned and beckoned. I sauntered toward her, swaying my hips. The sky seemed to lose all interest for her.

"It's all set then?" she asked when I was once again within her arms. I nodded. "Good. Then let's see this apartment of yours."

"What about you? I could be dangerous too," I said with a smirk.

"Someone already expects me by a certain time." She led me to the stairs down from the rooftop. Was she married? Partnered? I looked to her left hand, chastising myself for not doing so before. Her ring finger was empty.

She must have noticed. She laughed. "My cousin." She said, "I'm visiting and working here for a few months while she recovers from a brain transplant."

It was my turn to laugh. "A brain transplant?"

"Well...no. It was a knee replacement. She's terribly conservative and I was lost in wishful thinking."

Once we were inside the elevator, Lynn gently pinned me against the wall. "Don't get too comfortable." She gathered my wrists with one hand and collected a handful of my hair in the other. She kissed my throat, then my lips. "I'm still not happy that you embarrassed me."

The heels of Lynn's boots tapped on the hardwood floor as we entered my apartment. I stayed behind her at the door, throwing locks. "There's not much here..." I started to explain, then stopped.

Lynn silenced me with an upheld finger as she advanced into the main room. I took a step forward. "No," she stated flatly. "Stay where you are." I froze, clasped my hands in front of me and watched from the corner of my eyes as she entered my bathroom.

She returned, filing her fingernails, and stopped in front of me. Her eyes were stunning. Bands of blue danced with quick, nimble fingers waiting to steal cerulean from the sky or azure from sapphires.

Lynn was quiet. Her expression changed. Her eyebrows lifted. "Well?" she asked.

"I..." I stammered. I considered telling her that I was lost in her eyes for a moment but doubted that she would believe me. "Please forgive me, but would you repeat the question?" She scowled. Her hands found her hips. My gaze returned to the floor.

"I'm through imagining you without clothing," Lynn said in a matter-of-fact manner. "I don't want to have to rely on my daydreams any longer." Even though I kept my gaze on the floor I could tell Lynn had paused to look at me. I shuffled my feet.

"Strip."

"Yes, Lynn," I replied, and reached to untie my boots.

"Stop," she said, with much more emotion than her previous instruction. Half bent over, I froze. "I'm Ms. Lynn to you." She smiled. "Continue."

Anxiety, but also arousal, rose in me with each article of clothing I removed until I reached for the sides of my panties, when a delicious thought crossed my mind. I turned my back to Lynn and began playfully slithering out of them. I heard her chuckle as I kept my legs straight, bent at the waist and lowered my underwear very slowly to the ground.

"I'm going to enjoy this," Lynn said in a playful tone, as we moved into the bedroom. Then her voice became stern, as it had been on the roof when she asked about my BDSM questioning over lunch. "Kneel on the bed with your hands on the head-board. Do you have rope, scarves or a few belts? If so, where are they?"

"Yes, Ms. Lynn." I replied, "the rope is coiled beneath my bed. I've a single scarf wrapped around a vase in my closet. I've several belts in the bottom drawer of my dresser."

She nodded. "Don't move your hands." She coiled rope around my wrists and the headboard. "Do you have safewords?" she asked. I told her what they were and what they meant to me. She had me repeat them a few times.

"On a scale of one to ten," she asked, "How afraid are you right now?"

I shivered. "Until you asked that, two." I thought for a moment. "Now three, Ms. Lynn."

Then I felt her hand between my thighs. She slid her fingers along the lips of my sex. I moaned and shuddered with delight. She placed her other hand on my bum to steady me. "Easy pet," she said lovingly, "you're not to reach orgasm until I give you permission. Do you understand?"

"Yes, Ms. Lynn." I answered. It was a throaty whisper.

I all but squealed when she pressed a finger into me. She withdrew and giggled. I guessed that she hadn't expected such a response, but I'd been wet and aching since we'd left the drugstore. I begged her to continue.

"Are you always this mouthy?" she asked with a grin. When I responded by begging more, she cupped one of my breasts. I gasped. My pleading was replaced with whimpers and moans as she alternately rubbed and pinched my nipples. "Well," she said, "that seems to shut you up." I was about to nod and agree when she pinched my nipple hard between her nails.

Lynn released my poor nipple after I yelped. She chuckled a bit more before asking, "You're a bit loud for an apartment complex, don't you think?"

I first nodded yes. Then said, "No, Ms. Lynn." I didn't care so long as she touched me again. I wanted her soft hands all over me. "Does it matter?"

Lynn smiled widely. "Yes pet. It matters." She disappeared into my closet.

I whimpered and became a little frightened. For the first time it truly dawned on me that a stranger was in my apartment. We were alone, and I was bound.

Then Lynn returned with the scarf. I breathed a sigh of relief. I half smiled until she picked up the pair of panties I'd been wearing and I realized what she was doing. "This should shut you up," she said, just before wadding up the panties and stuffing them into my mouth. She waved a red-painted fingernail in front of my face. "Don't spit." I only looked at her with pleading eyes.

I didn't want to be gagged. It limited my speech. I couldn't communicate effectively. It objectified me. Yet when Lynn threaded the scarf through my teeth, under my hair and around my head, I could feel my sex throbbing. While she tied it tightly I could think of little else except the fact that I wanted to beg, and beg, and beg to be touched, but I could not. That seemed only to make my excitement more profound.

"There." She stepped back. "That's better." Then she lifted my black leather belt from the floor. The scarf around my head had not been the only thing she'd retrieved from my closet. I panted through my nose. I tried to plead but only tiny muffled sounds escaped the gag the devious blonde had constructed and strapped into my mouth.

The belt was lifted into the air and landed across my bum with a loud smack. It felt like I'd been stung by a dozen bees all at once. I pleaded into the gag. I showed puppy-dog eyes. I squirmed, but the rope around my wrists held.

"Pay attention," Lynn commanded. "You're not to speak of BDSM while in my presence." She lashed the belt across my rear again. Again the bees stung. Again I yelped into the gag.

"The only exception..." *Smack!* "...is if we are alone..." *Smack!* "...in either your apartment..." *Smack!* "...or my home." *Smack!* "Is that clear?" *Smack!*

I was already in tears. I sobbed a bit and nodded my head.

"I asked you a question," Lynn stated in a very agitated voice. I felt fear push its way through pain and embarrassment. They mingled in my belly, leaving me cold and hot all at once. I began to shake.

The belt came down across my bum again, harder this time. Bees turned to fire. I whined into the gag. I couldn't answer. How could she expect me to answer? I couldn't speak. I nodded my head up and down furiously.

She hit me again with the belt and flames raced through my nervous system. I screamed into the gag, "Yes, Ms. Lynn! It's clear! I understand!" but only muffled mewling escaped.

It was enough. She lowered the belt, and I felt a dam break inside me. I sobbed and shook.

Lynn grabbed a wad of toilet paper from my bathroom and returned. She'd taken off her boots, sweater and skirt. All she wore was a bra and a pair of panties. I wasn't sure when she had undressed or even how, but she was suddenly on the bed with me. She wrapped me in one arm and petted my hair. She kissed my tears away and wiped my nose with the soft toilet tissue, whispering in my ear the entire time, "Good girl. Good girl."

She untied the scarf and removed the panties from my mouth after I stopped shaking. I was embarrassed by a little string of drool that followed the panties but Lynn only smiled and wiped it away with the toilet tissue. I made a mental note to buy an industrial size box of Kleenex the next time I visited the store.

She began to untie me and I thanked her but she held one finger to her lips. I was mildly stunned but kept my mouth shut. I didn't want to be gagged again so soon. Why didn't she wish me to thank her?

I flexed my jaw until I was untied. She told me to fetch a glass of water. I did so and was ordered to drink it, then use the bathroom.

Lynn greeted me as I exited the bathroom. "I want you to undress me," she said. She was still wearing her lacy bra and panties, and I happily obliged. I opened my mouth to ask how she'd like me to do it but she held a finger to her lips again. I pouted but nodded my compliance.

I stepped behind her and tightly gripped the two halves of her bra strap. After unfastening them, I kept them together, easing them apart slowly so her breasts were not suddenly unsupported. I knew it could feel uncomfortable, as if someone had dropped them, if I were to take the bra off suddenly. That was the last thing I wished her to feel, so I eased it off slowly. Then I folded it and placed it atop her other clothing in the corner.

I knelt in front of her and everything else leapt out of mind. My sex ached. I could smell her. She was very excited, and I wanted nothing more than to taste her that very second. I thought of asking her if I could, but then remembered that she had shushed me twice. I guessed that she probably wouldn't shush me many more times before the belt or something worse became involved. So I looked up at her sex while I slid her panties slowly over her hips, down her thighs, over her shapely calves, and held them as she lifted one delicate foot at a time from them.

Lynn ordered me back onto the bed, on my back. I complied and was surprised when she climbed on the bed from the opposite direction. She straddled my face and hovered her sex just above my mouth. "Do I have your attention?"

I bit my lower lip to keep from agreeing verbally. How could she *not* have my attention? I nodded, remembering that she shushed me earlier. "Good," she continued. "Play with yourself while you take care of me. Give me a show, but you're not to orgasm before I do. Is that understood?" I nodded again and was rewarded when Lynn lowered her sex toward my mouth.

I could smell her. I wanted to taste her. I wanted to please her. I wanted to hear her shriek. I wanted her fingers tangled in my hair, to feel her dig fingernails into my shoulders and know that she did so because I gave her pleasure.

I closed my eyes, reached out with my tongue and found her warm to the touch. I heard a steady release of breath as her weight shifted and she settled over my mouth. Everything between my thighs tightened and for long minutes she rocked slightly back and forth over my mouth until her back arched and my sheets were gathered in her hands. I expected screams, but she seemed to contract in on herself with small sounds and sighs.

She sucked in a shuddering breath, lifted one leg, and fell on the bed at my left shoulder. I turned my gaze up to her hooded eyes. She licked her lips. "We're not quite finished, pet." I lifted an eyebrow and she laughed. "Fetch me a glass of water, my purse and your phone."

I blinked for a moment, then nodded and rolled off the bed, returning with all she requested.

The water vanished quickly. I felt a bit of pride in that. Then Lynn beckoned me with a nod of her head. When I drew close she held my face with both hands and kissed my cheek. "Now we're done. I want to stay, but my sister...she wouldn't understand."

A lump rose in my throat. "Oh, that pout!" Lynn reached forward and stroked my cheek with her fingertips. "I'll think of something. Besides, I'd like our next arrangement to include breakfast."

That lifted the corners of my mouth. "So there will be a next time?"

"Was there any doubt?" Lynn reached for her purse, pulled a phone from the inner recesses, and swung her feet from my bed. We dressed slowly and exchanged phone numbers.

She kissed me again, softly on the cheek, as she left. "Call if you don't hear from me by the weekend." She stared into my eyes. "Be discreet. Leave a message if I don't answer. I may be at the hospital."

I nodded and opened the door for her. She held up her phone and waggled it from side to side in her hand. "Don't forget your safe call." Then she was through the door, boots clicking down the hallway.

I closed the door and stood with my back against it for a long moment before lifting my phone. A familiar voice answered after the first ring. "No trouble?"

"None at all." I purred.

Laughter. "Glad to hear it. Need anything?"

"Just sleep and to rest my jaw."

More laughter. "Good. We'll see you this weekend?"

"Wouldn't miss it." I paused. "Thanks."

"Anytime. G'night, girly."

I tucked my phone away and turned toward my bedroom. I was alone for the night but knew the sheets would still smell of her.

BREATHE

Sommer Marsden

Social anxiety. Sucks to have it. If you've never experienced it, let me assure you it's not nearly as benign as it sounds. What starts as just a bright streak of panic through your insides can quickly bleed into a steady, whispering, crawling fear. Lurking just beneath the surface of your quite normal—quite sane-looking—façade.

Nick watches me when we go to these big parties. I often forget he's watching me, though. What with my mind and body screaming at me to leave this overcrowded, loud, bright situation or I might die, it's easy to lose track of things as simple as a glance. Even if Nick's glances are rarely simple.

I look up just in time to see him raise an eyebrow and step toward me. Then my new boss is there, right at my elbow, talking to me in a booming voice. This party is for him, after all. He's had the six glasses of champagne to prove it. He's a nice man, if slightly tipsy, but in this particular moment, trapped in my own personal hell, he might as well be Satan himself.

I only manage to catch the words "...good time, Glenna?" and I have enough presence of mind to realize he's asking me a question.

Before I can answer—it's hard to think with my head spinning—I feel the familiar commanding touch at my other elbow. Nick leans in and growls, "Breathe, Glenna."

And I do. I take a long, deep breath that rivals the coolest drink of water. I hold it as my heart pounds out four steady beats, then I blow it out in a hearty, even stream of air. I feel more sane. I feel more present. I smile at my new boss and say, "Fabulous time, Mr. Brick. You?"

"Good, good!" he brays, and then someone calls out to him and he smiles before flitting off, an oversized moth in a charcoal-gray suit, bouncing from the light of one guest to the next.

"Again," Nick says sharply. I realize that yes, again I've forgotten to breathe, so I obey.

Breathing is the first thing an anxious person forgets to do, and then they wonder why they feel as if they're drowning. Breathing is the first thing that Nick helped me with when our relationship went from part-time play-and-fuck-buddies to something more. He tells me what to do at times like this. I do it. It is as simple and perfect as that. A mystical symbiosis on which words would be lost.

"How much longer do you have in you, baby?" he asks. His face is a mask of easy amusement. He nods to people as they pass and call greetings. Raises his glass—whiskey neat—to a woman we know from not just my workplace but our gym.

All of these people I can take on a one-on-one basis. Even in a very small group. But fuck me, if you put them all in one room in a party situation and expect a festive mood...panic ensues.

"A half hour? Maybe." I gave up on feeling bad or embarrassed about this problem of mine ages ago. Right around the time I met Nick. I used to let it eat at me and once even considered drugs to deal with it. Now, I try to expose myself to the situation as much as possible and hope I will gradually adjust. But I have limits. I'm reaching them now.

"Let's say thirty minutes, then," he says, kissing the side of my neck and pressing a warm hand to the small of my back. The touch is promising. I'm being informed of what awaits me if I make it through those endless thirty minutes.

And right there in the midst of the blaring sound and light and flashing chaos of what you'd call a party, I feel a rush of sticky, wet heat between my legs. I can tell right then that my panties will be damp when they are removed by this man. That my legs will shake a bit and my hands will tremble and I'll be on the verge of orgasm before he even touches me.

Those thirty minutes last a lifetime. Even with his hand splayed on my back. Even with his breath rushing over my face as he murmurs in my ear. I drink my wine, grateful that it does help the clawing anxiety in my chest a bit. I used to drink more of it for the effect, but then found myself apprehensive *and* a bit drunk. No fun.

"You really have won the prize of prizes," Jenny from the mailroom says, nodding to Nick as he wanders off for a refill.

He's left me to test me, and I vow to do well. I lick my lips and try to focus on Jenny. Just Jenny. Only Jenny. My mind struggling to block out the swirling, whirling party on the periphery of my vision. "Yes, I did."

"I bet he's a master in the sack," she laughs.

She's being funny—it's a good-natured joke—but before I can catch myself, I say, "Yes. He is."

And everywhere else too... my mind supplies.

I blush.

Then again, so does Jenny and she nudges me saying, "Go, Glenna..." slyly.

I laugh softly and forget, for that moment in time, my fears. It's just me and Jenny, just like at work. We often chat and joke and drink a cup of coffee while we pretend to sort mail. I'm a girl Friday. I flit from place to place in the company and am useful where I'm needed.

Nick says it's my talent. I'm a valuable chameleon. The first time he said it I knew I loved him. Because it was how I felt about my often-belittled job.

"And here he comes. With lust in his eyes," Jenny says in my ear. She nudges me again and I actually giggle. "Someone's getting laid tonight."

"Gosh," I say, jokingly. "I hope it's me."

"I don't think you have to worry about that."

Then his hand is against my spine, one finger slinking slowly beneath the low-cut back of my dress. "Ready to go as soon as I finish this?" he asks me, smiling at Jenny as he says it. Jenny is blushing too. He has that effect on most women.

"I am," I say. I try to make my voice sound strong and normal. To my own ears I simply sound grateful.

"I'm impressed," he says as we drive. He puts a hand in my lap—possessively. He squeezes my mound once, but doesn't push up under my dress. I pray for him to touch me, but he simply lets his hand go soft over my sex.

"Thank you."

"You almost seemed to be enjoying yourself at the end," he says.

"I was. Jenny was joking with me and for a second it all bled away. All the too-bright, too-loud, too-much sensations faded."

"What were you talking about?" He turns left onto Crenshaw Boulevard and my heart picks up. We are getting closer and closer to home. To bed. To reward.

"You," I say, and put my head down, for some reason feeling shy.

He chuckles and surprises me by sliding that hand up under my dress the way I'd hoped. His finger works easily beneath my panties and he slips it deep inside my cunt. The way he's touching me, he has to press the palm of his hand to the top of my mons. It adds a delicious pressure that wrings a moan out of me even as he slows the car. "I'm proud of you. That's my girl. And how wet are you? I'd say very," he says, answering his own question.

Then he waggles that finger enough to make my pulse jackhammer in my temples before withdrawing and pressing my dress neatly back into position.

Both hands on the wheel, he guides us the rest of the way home.

My stockings whisper as I take the stairs quickly, gripping his hand and following his lead. He points to the bed, and I sit. He doesn't need to speak to me, and I don't need to hear his voice to understand. I understand perfectly. There's a bond here. Something a lot of people might not understand. Which makes it even more thrilling, I have to admit.

His hands are steady and sure as he takes off his tie and drapes it on the chair. Button by button he opens his shirt and removes it. Next his dress pants. His socks. His shoes.

Then he's standing in front of me, hand on my chin, tilting it up so that I must look past his hard cock, his flat stomach, his strong chest and up to his face. He smiles at me and something tight in me loosens, something cold in me warms.

"Open," he says, and it's barely a whisper.

I part my lips and sigh softly as he plays the tip of his cock—
silken and warm—along my lower lip. I don't dart my tongue out
like I want to; I'll do that if instructed. For now, I sit and breathe
in the rich smell of him—cologne, body heat and cold air.

He slips into my mouth a little bit at a time, playing with me.
I allow my jaw to inch open as he pushes forward, and then his
skin is no longer a scent but a taste.

When he's fully seated in my mouth, stretching my jaw
wide, he wraps one hand around my throat and squeezes gently.
Just enough for me to feel the struggle and pull that signal the
need for air. He thrusts deep, puts a bit more pressure on my
thin throat and then lets up. "Breathe," he says, and I do. The
moment I'm sated, his hand tightens a bit more.

It's the way I feel when I'm anxious. That need for air, that
craving. And yet in his hands the same sensation is a riot of
arousal and lust. It's good when he's the one denying me air and
not my own blind fear.

Trickles of air make it in, filling my nose weakly to slip down
my air passages. I feel buzzy but not frantic. I feel peaceful and
focused. His hand relaxes.

"Breathe." I do and his hand tightens again, but not as much.
And then he says: "Touch yourself."

I bunch up my dress, scurrying and scrambling to get my
hands beneath the fabric that seems to have mysteriously tripled
in volume in the last few minutes. My seeking fingers find my
panties and force their way down inside them. My fingers on my
clit are not without a tremor. I stroke myself and moan softly
around his thrusting cock. His hand grips a bit tighter, stifling
that moan and killing it softly.

My fingers pluck and pinch at my clit, and my body grows
tighter. When Nick pulls free of my mouth, I forget my manners
for a second and chase after him with my tongue.

"Glenna," he says sharply, and withdraws his hand. I feel the absence of his grip on my neck.

"Sorry," I say quickly. "I'm sorry."

"Get yourself off," he says, moving away, leaning back against the dresser like he's watching a stage play.

Blush heats my face and I obey him, feeling a burst of gratitude that the room is only lit by a dimly glowing lamp. Fingers slick and skating as I stroke my pussy, I play languidly as he watches because I know he likes it. He gives me a half grin knowing that I'm missing the feel of his fingers curled to my throat.

I push two fingers inside myself, grind against my palm, flex my fingers to the plump engorged G-spot, and when he smiles at me and nods, I come.

I sit there, breathless, fingers wet, body flexing deep inside with the aftershocks of my pleasure.

Nick moves toward me slowly so my eyes have a chance to track every single step he takes. He pushes me back roughly. This is not sweet and tender lovemaking. This is not prom night. This isn't romance. This is what I need, fucking and writhing and the feel of him deciding when I can draw a big gulp of air and when I can't.

This is about trust. Utter, blind belief in another person's ability to dictate what you can and cannot do. This is freedom.

My back hits the bed, my long brown hair fanning out and a bit of it falling forward to cover my eyes. He brushes it away with a firm flick of his hand. He likes to look into my eyes. He likes to watch me watching him, submitting to him.

"Breathe," he says again.

I take a deep breath and then feel the start of his fingers pressing to my neck, trapping my thumping pulse beneath his thick fingertips.

With his free hand he shoves my panties down and knocks my legs wide. The breath I do have startles in my lungs, making me feel as if I have a frantic bird trapped in my chest. My cunt goes slicker, warmer, needier, and I feel my own moisture in a rush along the top of my thighs.

He tests me with a finger, laughs, pushes the head of his cock to me and plunges in. I grunt, body thrusting up on its own as his fingers bite against the tendons in my neck.

My eyes flash with violet, pink and white spots and I'm glad again the glow from the lamp is low so I can see the light show.

His cock fills me, driving deep, and I feel as if he might split me in half the way he's fucking me. Just when I think I might beg, he loosens his fingers and says it again.

"Breathe."

I suck in a sultry rush of air, and the world sharpens into focus. His fingers contract again and he rolls his hips back and forth before thrusting back into me. His free hand shoves under my ass, tilting me back for a better angle.

Every driving motion of his body brushes my clitoris with the base of his cock. That hard knot of bone there at his pelvis pushes me to the point of coming again, and when he lets up on his fingers I draw in air as my cunt grows tighter around him, milking him.

His grip resumes, harder than before. Restricting me so that I hear the rush-hiss-thump of blood in my ears, and I move up under him mindlessly. I'm sweating in my dress, the place between my breasts a damp, pounding hollow.

His dark eyes are studying me and he squeezes a bit harder though I'm ready for a breath.

This time he says, "Come."

And I do. The first blissful, sweeping arc of orgasm slams into me and he denies me just one more second, before releasing my throat and letting the delicious rush of air into my body. I arch up like I'm dying, grip at him, tug and pull as the spasms seem to go on for so much longer than normal. My head is languid and light, my body thrumming with blood. My pulse seems to be everywhere at once.

He puts his hands on my cheeks, still thrusting strong and deep. When he comes he kisses me, crying out against my lips, this time filling me with air instead of denying me.

I inhale the sound of his pleasure and push my hands to his warm skin. He drops to his side and gathers me in so I'm tangled up around him, my hair spread across his arm, his chest. In the house it's quiet, no sound but our breathing.

WHAT'S NOT
TO LIKE?

D. L. King

B ack from a late lunch, I usher you inside and make coffee. I
need to talk to you, I say, because we're such good friends.
You sit on the couch and give me your earnest attention.

I am Dan's slave. I know; it's not something you'd expect to
hear from me. Believe me, it's not something I ever expected
to hear myself say. But really, how could I not be after all the
things he's taught me—all the things he's done for me—all the
things he's done *to* me?

We met innocently enough. Well, you know. You introduced
us at that dinner party, a year ago. You seated us together; you
must have meant for something to happen. No, I'm not blaming
you; I'm thanking you.

We talked all through dinner. He was smart, sweet, even
deferential, or so it seemed. He had a passion for his work, and
I could tell he was very good at it. Neither of us wanted the
evening to end, and so we left the party together. He walked me
home, and I invited him in for a glass of port. One thing led to
another, and we wound up in bed.

He took charge, but not in a way I couldn't handle. His fingers explored every inch of me, caressing and prodding. He easily shifted me from side to side and turned me over when he wanted. I found it sexy—to be handled like that. He stroked my breasts from base to tip, using a lot of pressure, letting his fingers come to points at the nipple, pulling them outward, elongating them, over and over. That alone got me wet, but when those same beautiful, long fingers began to caress my pussy and pull at my labia, I practically gushed into his hands.

"So responsive." That's what he said, practically under his breath. "So responsive." And then he plunged into my cunt, making my back arch and the breath leave my lungs. He fucked me hard, all the gentleness gone, and I came at least three times before he reached his climax.

He pulled out and removed the spent condom. "Marta, would you mind?" he asked, holding it out to me.

"Oh, sure," I said. I guess I was a bit taken aback, but it seemed like the natural thing to do. Before I made my way back from the bathroom after getting rid of his condom, I stopped and wet a washcloth with warm water to bring back to him. I found him propped up against the headboard, on top of the covers, one leg slightly bent at the knee and the other straight out. I held the cloth out to him.

"That was very thoughtful, Marta." He took it and quickly cleaned himself up, before handing the used washcloth back to me. "Thank you. Take care of that and then come back here." It seemed like an order, but it also seemed like a reasonable request. When I came back again, he was in the same position. He reached for my wrist and pulled me down to him, so he could kiss me. When he let my wrist go, I stood back up and saw this virtual stranger, this man, Dan, lounging naked on my bed, looking every inch the master of it. "I'd like to see you again," he said. "I think we have a lot in common."

For my part, I couldn't have agreed more. I was jumping up and down inside and couldn't wait to feel those fingers on me again but, trying to be cool, I said, "Yes, I think that would be nice." Picking up my panties from the floor, I started to put them on.

"Oh, don't get dressed," he said. "You look so beautiful naked."

I smiled and dropped the panties and watched him dress. When he was fully dressed and I was still naked, he wrapped his arm around my waist, pulling me to him, pressing me against the closed zipper of his jeans. He held me to him and lowered his mouth to mine while his hand moved down my ass and slid between my legs to grab my cunt, which was wet again. "Mmm, yes, very responsive. I'll call you."

It seemed like forever before he called me, but it was only a couple of days. We started dating. He took me to dinner, to the theater; we watched TV at my house, always followed by great sex. It wasn't like any kind of sex I'd known before; it was singular to him. His dominance, his manipulation of my body, put me in a completely new mind-set. I craved his touch. I would do anything to have it. He told me to get my pubic hair waxed off. Of course I did it right away.

We'd been seeing each other for about two months when he invited me to his apartment for a home-cooked meal. I was excited—because he wanted to cook for me, but also because I would finally get to see where he lived.

"Wear that little black dress I like so much," he'd said.

"Okay."

"But don't wear any underwear."

It was the first time he'd asked me to do that. I thought about saying no, but didn't know why I would. I thought about ignoring the request but realized it was an order, and I said, after just the tiniest of lag time, "Okay."

I tried not to think about it, but all the way over, I was afraid my dress would end up showing my arousal for all to see. Dan lives in a penthouse apartment in Midtown. He's a very successful engineer, but no engineer makes that much money. He has family money. I couldn't wait to see his place, and it didn't disappoint. Huge by Manhattan standards, it had a roof deck with entrances from the bedroom and the living room. With an address in the fifties and facing downtown, the views were spectacular. He gave me a peck on the cheek and took me on a tour. The living room was practically as big as my one-bedroom apartment in Brooklyn. There was a dining room and a big open kitchen. He took me out on the deck to show off his potted garden and barbecue space and then into the bedroom from the deck. The king-size bed and modern, clean lines of his furniture made me want to stay here, at least for a while, but he took me by the hand and led me out into the hall, pointing out the bathroom, the guest room, the entertainment room with huge flat screen and sound system and then he stopped.

"This is my playroom." He opened the door. Royal-blue, deep-pile carpeting covered the floor, and the walls were painted a pale gray-blue. There was a window with an uptown view, but because he was so high up, there were no neighboring apartments to look into. Another king-size bed, this one with brushed steel posts and canopy, dominated the space. The room was obviously meant to be another bedroom and had a closet and attached bath. There were bed tables on each side of the bed with lamps, and a Chinese black-lacquer chest at the foot of the bed. There were three other pieces of furniture in the room: a blue-velvet club chair, a dark wood X-shaped monstrosity in the corner and another piece of dark wood and leather furniture I couldn't identify.

"Well, all right," I said. I knew a kinky sex room when I saw one. Actually, I didn't, but I'd read that *Fifty Shades of Grey* book and wasn't an idiot. "Let's play, then."

"After dinner," he said, and ushered me out the door and back into the dining room. He brought me a glass of wine and said, "We're almost ready to eat, I just want to check something first. From behind me, he put an arm around my waist and as I leaned back against him, he slid his other hand under my skirt and stroked my recently dampened, unpantied pussy. "Good girl," he said. He smoothed my skirt back down and went back into the kitchen, licking his fingers.

I could feel my face reddening and my temperature rising. *I should be insulted by that,* I thought, *so why am I so turned on?* All through dinner I fidgeted and squirmed, thinking about the playroom and what we might do there. I have no idea what we ate. I knew the meal was concluded when he said, "I don't think you need that anymore, do you?" touching the sleeve of my dress. "Take it off and go hang it up in the closet in the playroom."

He was always polite, and I always felt that I could have said no at any time, but he never actually *asked* me to do anything; he always *told* me and, somehow, that just seemed right. I stood up from the table and lifted my dress over my head and turned toward the hallway. He followed me into the room.

The closet had a very small clothes rack, with a few hangers. It was mostly filled with rows of hooks from which hung various whips, paddles and floggers and shelving units which held a plethora of other items, most—probably all—of a sexual nature, though I didn't have a clue what some of them were.

"Hmm," I said. He was standing directly behind me. He

reached both hands around my thighs and spread the lips of my pussy open while he stroked the insides with his thumbs.

"I already know you're sexually submissive." I squirmed in his hands. "No, you know you are. But I think you might also make an excellent slave." I pulled away from him. He caught me and spun me around to face him. "No, I think it's something you were made for. Or at least something you and I were made for, together."

We talked about it together, I naked, and he clothed. He sat me on the odd-shaped piece of furniture and pulled up the club chair and told me about submission and slavery and how they were different. He told me about the things he'd like to do to me and with me. Early in the discussion, he placed his hands on my knees and spread my legs. He told me to keep my hands behind me. Occasionally, as he would explain certain things to me, he'd reach over and insert a finger or two inside me, or squeeze my clit, just to check my arousal, he said. Of course I just got wetter and wetter.

I asked him what I was sitting on and he said it was a spanking bench. I asked him how it worked and he showed me how to lie astride it, on the padded-leather top. He placed my knees and shins on the padded beam running along each side that I'd previously been using as a footrest. Then he walked round behind me and pulled me toward him a bit. That left my cunt free and open to his use. He placed my hands on handles in front of my knees.

"Comfy?"

"Yeah, I am," I said. "But I don't like being spanked."

"Oh, I think I can change your mind about that," he said, and proceeded to spank me with his bare hand. Occasionally, he'd stop spanking and play in my dripping pussy, and then he'd go back to spanking. He began easy. It didn't hurt. But shortly after he began the spanks got harder and harder, until I was grunting and shrieking with each new application of his hand. At one point, I reached around to cover my ass and he grabbed my wrist and held it to the small of my back. He stopped spanking long enough to collect the other wrist and grip them both together. Then he gave me three very hard spanks.

"Stop, stop, stop," I said.

He stopped spanking me, but put two fingers in my cunt and began to fuck me with them. "Those last spanks were punishment for trying to cover your bottom. I won't have you hide yourself from me." He fucked me slowly while he talked to me, explaining the rules. "Most often, I'll fasten your wrists and ankles to the bench so you can't move them, but I just wanted to give you a little taste." He continued to finger-fuck me, my body slowly building toward orgasm. "I think you liked it. Did you like it?"

I felt a bit like a wet dishrag, but I managed to croak out, "Yes, god yes," as my ass bounced up against his hand, trying to drive his fingers as far inside me as possible.

"Such a greedy little cunt you are." He removed his fingers and just as I groaned at the loss of them, I felt a sharp smack right against my swollen lips and clit. My mind exploded as my body convulsed in what was possibly the most intense orgasm I'd experienced, up to that time.

"Fuck me!" I said.

"Is that an exclamation or an invitation?" he asked.

"I think it was an exclamation," I said, "though, if you give me a minute, you could take it as an invitation, too."

That was my introduction to submission and the possibilities of slavehood. And believe me, I've had even more intense orgasms since then. Remember when I said he was a brilliant engineer? Well, he *is* a brilliant engineer. He's designed and built a few interesting devices and furnishings for his playroom, all specifically tailored to me and my measurements. He says he dreamed about the latest piece—woke up with a screaming hard-on, too. After he fucked me, he went right to his drafting table and came up with this most ingenious piece of furniture. And like all his various torture devices, it's amazingly comfortable.

You see, the shoulder harness pops up and I step up and slide right in. This piece here keeps my knees spread and resting on the padded leather blocks and my back supported by the padded leather backrest. It's even got lumbar support. The shoulder harness comes down, holding me against the supports, and I recline backward a bit, into the neck and headrest. There are two attached leather straps, one for my chin and one for my forehead. They keep my head in position. Now my mouth and throat are at the perfect height and angle for Master's cock. We worked at it, together, to get just the right angle, both comfortable for me and the perfect fit for him. I think it's my favorite new piece of furniture, and as you can see, he's made several. It has attachments, too. Look. He can attach various dildos and vibrators to keep either my cunt or my ass filled, or both, if he wants. Again, the angle is perfect for my holes, so everything fits just right.

Sometimes he fastens me in and doesn't fuck my mouth at all but just plays with me. As much as I love his cock in my mouth, sometimes I like the way he plays with me even more. He can use his beautiful fingers to torment my nipples. He can attach weights to them and to my pussy lips. He even has an attachment that can clamp and keep my nipples stretched as far as they'll go. He can torment me in so many ways; make me come over and over again. You see, he loves to watch me come. He'll make me come over and over until he's ready to take me. The only drawback to this particular piece is that he can only fuck my mouth. If he wants to fuck my ass or my cunt, he has to take me out of it. But there are other pieces he's made that are designed for that kind of fucking. It just takes a little planning ahead.

So now you understand why I choose to be Dan's slave. He loves me and I would do anything he asks because I know he'd never ask for anything I couldn't give. He keeps me well taken care of and safe, and I wouldn't want anything else. I can see you're getting a little turned on. Dan'll be home soon. He wanted me to invite you over and show you around. He'd like you to stay for dinner, if you want. It'll give us a chance to chat and catch up. You won't mind if I get out of these clothes, will you? I'm not allowed to wear them inside.

HELL-BENT
FOR LEATHER

Victoria Behn

Struggling beneath the weight of three bags of groceries, a brick-heavy handbag and an unwieldy set of keys, Melissa slammed the car door shut with her backside. Her leather jacket had been the wrong choice today. Rain slid behind her collar, down her cheeks and into her shoes. The wind whipped her hair into her eyes and the skinny handles of the plastic bags pressed into her palms, leaving deep red lines.

After dropping the keys on the welcome mat and cursing to herself, she managed to find the lock in the dark. The front door swung open, banging against the small table at the foot of the stairs. A pile of unopened letters fell to the floor. She kicked the door shut and threw the keys onto the table. Light fell across the upstairs landing, and the gentle thud of drums seeped through the bedroom floor. Of course. He was "working" from home today.

Melissa kicked her shoes under the table and let her handbag drop onto the carpet. Her stockings were wet around the toes.

She felt a muscle twang painfully in her right shoulder as she maneuvered the heavy bags the last few feet toward the kitchen. As she put the bags on the counter a jar of pasta sauce slipped off the work surface and fell to the tiled floor. It didn't bounce. Her feet were now smothered in dark-red tomato pulp and small, dangerous slivers of glass.

Upstairs, the music continued but she heard the sound of the bedroom door opening, followed by footsteps on the stairs.

"Stand still." Al was looking over the banister.

"It's okay—I'll get it."

She leaned over to reach for a cloth from the sink, but he stepped up behind her and caught her hand.

"I said stand still."

Al placed his hands on her taut shoulders, standing behind her, and she felt his hot breath on the top of her head as he inhaled the scent of her hair before exhaling with a deep sigh.

"I don't want you to get hurt."

He ran his hot fingers beneath the damp collar of her jacket and gently pulled it down, around her shoulders and away from her arms. She heard the sound of it hitting the floor in the hallway, where he'd thrown it. Al's hands went back up to Melissa's head as he ran his fingers over her forehead, wiping away the rain. He took half a step closer, so that she felt his belt buckle against her hip. His fingers slid down her temples, stroked each cheek and then one hand firmly held her chin while he used the forefinger of the other to push into her mouth. Melissa gasped as he pushed one, two, then three of his broad fingers between her teeth and into the back of her throat, stretching her lips and coating his fingers in her saliva. Just as quickly, he withdrew his hands so that she was left with her mouth open and her breath quick as she stood in a pool of sauce.

"Hands behind your head."

Melissa hesitated. She could feel goose pimples tracking up her arms. She needed to get out of her damp clothes, and she needed to put the groceries away.

"Honey, there's ice cream and frozen chicken. I need to put these things away, and then I've a pile of planning to do for the new case. Jill wants to go over the preliminary report tomorrow and I haven't even read the damned thing yet because—"

Everything became smudged as she viewed the kitchen through the tight weave of Al's shirt, which had just been thrown over her face. The sound of her breathing was intensified as the fabric moved in and out against her lips and her nostrils filled with the heavy, musky scent of Al's sweat. She felt the shirtsleeves tighten into a knot at the back of her head. Melissa put her hands up to her face to remove it, laughing, but Al's hands grabbed her wrists tightly and pulled them up behind her neck.

"I don't like having to repeat myself. I get it. You've had a tough day. You're tired. You're stressed." She was aware that he was holding her wrists with one hand while he removed his belt with the other. "I felt your shoulders. Tight." He pulled her wrists together so that they formed a cross and he wound his belt carefully around them, making sure to twist it both ways so that she couldn't simply wriggle free. "Like I said, I don't want you to get hurt."

These last words were whispered close to her ear. Melissa felt the first hot pulse of liquid soaking into her underwear. The chill from the rain meant that her nipples were already pert beneath the cream lace bra. But now she was drawn to the sensations of that rigidness as the nerves became more sensitive. Suddenly she longed to thrust them toward his fingers, toward his mouth. She toyed with the idea of misbehaving—acting out of turn. This would almost certainly earn her a punishment of some description. But she was tired. She didn't know how much punishment she could take tonight.

"Lean forward."

Melissa had little difficulty in obeying as Al's hand pushed hard on the top of her back, forcing her into a vulnerable position. She had to keep her feet perfectly still among the spilled sauce and broken glass on the floor. At the same time her center of balance had shifted. The partial blindness was disorienting, and having her hands tied behind her neck meant she couldn't steady herself. She wobbled to the side and let out a small cry in case she fell. Al's hands shot out to her shoulders. He held them tightly while he pushed his now-hard cock against her backside. She could feel the heat of his arousal through the thin fabric of her skirt.

Once she was steady, Al's hands left her shoulders and his fingers ran down each side of her spine. She arched her back to meet his touch, but his hands kept moving over her buttocks. One hand moved farther down, between her legs, into her slit. He rubbed his fingers into her cunt—slowly back and forth, forcing the juices to seep down through the cotton of her panties. As he toyed with her clit, his other hand pushed her skirt up, over her backside and onto her back. She felt his fingers pulling at the elastic of her wet panties and forcing them down, past her thighs and around her ankles.

"Hum me a tune," he told her.

Again Melissa wondered whether to disobey. She was sure it would earn her a quick spanking, and at this stage she wanted to be disciplined. The bondage, the blindfold, the instruction— it wasn't enough. To fully immerse herself in the moment, to forget the outside world, she needed pain. She suddenly felt a little less tired. She decided to misbehave. Melissa shook her head. The room became very quiet. Al's hands were removed from her body. She heard his footsteps behind her as he left the room.

She mustn't move now, that was key. The temptation to straighten up and ease the ache in her back and legs from holding the awkward position remained.

But that would be a bad idea.

Upstairs, Al walked into the bedroom. Alongside the sound of his music, she heard his footsteps on the wooden floorboards and the noise of a cupboard door being slammed shut. He came running down the stairs at speed and she heard the unmistakable sound of a leather belt striking the radiator in the hall. Her slit became hot and soaking, and the tips of her swollen breasts ached.

When he stood before her she saw, through the fabric of his shirt, it was not one leather belt. He held three.

Al's eager hands began to unfasten the buttons of her blouse, pulling it up and over her bound hands and head so that her torso was exposed. Next he unfastened the bra and pulled that out of the way. Barely any of her flesh remained covered. One of the belts slid across the top of her tits. The metal of the buckle was cold as he pulled it tight across her back. The second belt was pulled beneath her tits. The sensation of another buckle being pulled into place came ratchet-like across her spine. The binding was almost unbearably restrictive around her chest and her tits began to swell between the leather straps until they were painfully engorged.

Al reached round under her chest and squeezed each nipple until she cried out.

"That's not very tuneful is it?"

She felt him straighten up again so that his cock was up against her hip. He was standing sideways to her now.

"Now."

He demanded her obedience and she complied this time, beginning to hum something gentle, a little like a lullaby. She heard the swish of the leather through the air and flinched before the belt slapped across her flesh with a loud crack. The humming became a yelp but she quickly returned to the tune. A little pain was desirable, but a lot of pain would turn it into a feat of endurance.

Al's hand raised a second time, and she heard the leather rush to meet her flesh. She moaned this time, somewhere between a sound of surprise and delight, as the hot patch on her backside was revisited. She knew he couldn't resist bringing it down again in the same spot. He'd keep going until there was a mark. Part of the game was leaving a mark that he could admire later. Often it would be the recognition of this mark in the bedroom the next day that led them to their next encounter.

Ten lashes in all.

He was a fan of the decimal system.

Five to each cheek, for symmetry.

She continued to hum. Her backside was stinging and her cunt cried hot tears. Her pussy was achingly swollen now. She longed to feel him inside her. She pushed herself up against him but he crouched down beside her and carefully pulled her feet out of her stockings and panties, helping her to step backward onto a clean towel, away from the mess on the floor. He moved around behind her and she felt his breath on her anus for a moment before he moved in to lap at the flow of juice that was running down her thighs. He chased the drops up to their source, pushing his face into her cunt while he held her steady by grabbing the leather straps around her tits. The edge of the belts gripped the swollen flesh even tighter. She moaned again as the already cruel bindings cut deeper.

Here too, there would be marks.

Al's tongue pushed hard into her cunt and worked its way around inside her before retracting and moving up toward her clit. He teased it by circling gently round and round.

She groaned with pleasure and rocked back onto his face. The blood rushed into the walls around her cunt, which was now swollen with pleasure and beginning to pulsate. Given another minute of this she would climax, she was certain.

"Enough." The word was muffled between her legs as Al pulled away quickly.

He stood up and grabbed Melissa's hands, pulling her upright. He placed one arm around her waist and one around her shoulders and lifted her up, holding her against his body until she was out of the kitchen. He then proceeded to drag her through the hallway so that she was stumbling across the carpet. When they reached the bottom of the stairs he turned her around so he could pull her backward up the stairs.

By this stage she imagined her tits must be blue.

When they reached the landing, he let her go. She stood, cold and nervous, at the top of the stairs. She heard him walk into her study and take something from the desk. The next thing she was aware of was the plastic of a pair of pegs as he attached them to her nipples. Not content with simply gripping them, he began to twist them back and forth as she moaned quietly.

"Shut up."

He put a hand to her mouth and pulled the shirt up over her face. Tucking the edge up against her eyes, he leaned forward and licked her mouth. His hands reached down between her legs. His fingers moved into her cunt and came out sodden. Al reached back up toward her face and forced his fingers, wet with her juice, into her mouth. He pushed one, two, three, four fingers into her mouth so that her lips were spread wide and tight. Then he wiped the remaining juice across her face and put both hands on her shoulders and pushed her to her knees.

There was no prize for guessing what was coming now.

As he pulled his tightly swollen cock out of his pants, she could smell the metallic precome and the deeper notes of testosterone-infused sweat. She felt a few drops of the hot, clear liquid on her cheek as he pressed it into her face.

"Open wide."

She held her mouth open as wide as she could manage.

"Wider."

She tried again, sensing her jaw loosening at the hinge as she pressed her tongue to the base of her mouth. Finally, he seemed satisfied and the tip of his cock, soft and warm against her bottom lip, slid inside. Her lips moved to meet him as he pushed it farther into her mouth. She was crammed full of his length as he pushed deeper, coming up against the back of her throat so that she wanted to retch.

He stopped.

He held his cock motionless in her mouth.

She held her mouth still, keeping her teeth away from his flesh, pushing her tongue up against him. Unswallowed saliva began to pool behind her front teeth.

Slowly, Al began to move his cock in and out of her mouth. An excess of drool ran down her bottom lip. It cooled as it dripped down onto her tits. She moaned quietly, allowing the vibrations of her sigh to run up his length. His cock became even more engorged, and he reached around the back of her neck to release her hands.

"Balls."

Melissa pushed her hands between his legs. Her fingers were a little clumsy and numb from the belt. She could feel the lines around her wrists. More marks, but these would soon disappear.

Carefully, she encircled the base of his balls with her fingers and then squeezed firmly.

His cock surged as he pushed it into her throat.

"And the back."

She moved her hands again so that she was using just one hand to hold his balls tight. She forced a couple of fingers of her other hand into her mouth, along with his cock, to moisten them before reaching between his legs to locate his anus.

"Wait."

He pulled out of her mouth and she was left kneeling alone in the hallway for a moment before he returned and dragged her to her feet. She was pulled into the bedroom and pushed back onto the bed. He lifted her feet up and pushed her thighs apart so that her flesh was exposed, making the sheets damp. She heard the irresistible sound of the electric massager and her cunt salivated, Pavlovian style.

"Be quick now, the ice cream's melting."

He placed the buzzing head of the equipment against her clit and the hot waves of pleasure shot across her pelvis and up her back. She squirmed in delight and shuddered as her slit tightened again and again. Al placed one, then two, then three fingers inside her and began to tease her tightening cunt. He slid his fingers in and out while he pushed the massager harder against her clit.

Melissa reached around to find his cock. He was kneeling beside her now, intent on making her come. His breath was quick and she knew he was close.

"Leave it," he instructed her. "I want to come inside you when you're nice and tight."

Finally, Melissa submitted to the release. All she knew in the world was that hot space between her legs. She was brimming with the delight of an intensity far surpassing what she could achieve alone. As she came she moaned. He immediately removed his fingers from her cunt, climbing over her and thrusting his cock into that hot, tight space. He took the massager from her clit and reached up to twist the pegs on her nipples, causing a fresh wave of pleasure to wash across her groin.

It was a tight fit inside her now. He pushed in deep, increasing speed as he moved closer to his own climax. She continued to moan as she thrust against him, reaching back down to encircle his balls again. She felt the surge of his come as he too could resist the urge no longer. He pulled out of her deftly and splashed his come as far as it would go, up across her leather-lashed tits, over her neck and onto her face.

Finally, Al rolled her over so that he could remove the belts and the blindfold. He turned her onto her back again and kissed her full on her come-covered lips.

"That ice cream should be about right now, what do you think?"

"Yum?" she replied, wiping the wetness from her chest before licking it off her fingers.

"What makes you think you're getting any?" He gave her nipples a final tweak each before removing the pegs. "You didn't do as you were told."

Al pushed himself up from the bed and went downstairs.

Melissa pulled the blankets about her, nestling down into their warmth. She could hear the sounds of Al going into the kitchen, finding the ice cream and taking two spoons from the cutlery drawer.

PASSING THE FINAL

Donna George Storey

S he'd always done well on exams, but this one was different. There was no reviewing of notes or practice questions. She was simply to prepare herself as if for a date she knew would end in bed—a little extra perfume in secret places and sexy underwear—and report to his house at nine o'clock sharp. Of course she did exactly as she was told.

Her stomach clutched sweetly as his eyes flicked up and down her body.

"You look lovely. Now go into the bedroom, take off your dress and put on the robe on the bed. Then lie down and wait for me." His tone was as neutral as a beige ceiling, but her pulse leaped. This was how their games always began.

His bedroom was illuminated only by two thick, round candles arranged on the nightstand as if it were an altar. A satin robe lay shimmering in the golden shadows across the pillow. She hung her dress in his closet, kicked off her shoes and slipped the robe over her lacy, bride-white bra, matching thong and thigh-high stockings. She paused to check her reflection in the closet mirror.

Don't be afraid. The Master said you were ready.

He hadn't elaborated exactly what she was ready for, but she would find out soon enough. For some reason he'd removed his quilt and flat sheet, but fortunately the room was quite warm. She stretched out on the bed, realizing she'd never been here without him beside, above or below her.

A dark figure entered the room.

The Master.

He glided over and sat at the edge of the bed. His fingers brushed her hair as if he were comforting a sick child. "How are you feeling, Laura?"

"A little scared, Sir," she admitted.

"You'll pass with flying colors."

Her belly churned with curiosity—*Goddammit already, what are you going to make me do tonight?*—but the Master invariably punished ill-timed questions.

He smiled. "You've been a patient girl. I appreciate that. I'll explain the specifics of your final exam in due time. But first let me say how pleased I am with the progress you've made. When we first met you were too inhibited to reveal your true sensual nature to a man. Together we've watched your erotic response blossom, test by test. Now, my dear, I'd have to call you positively shameless in bed. I keep waiting for you to lose your nerve, but you never do."

She felt her body flushing, half in embarrassment, half in pleasure at his praise.

"However, there is one crucial weakness in your development." He paused and tilted his head. "Do you love me, Laura?"

"Of course, Sir. You know I how much I do," she faltered,

confused. He never spoke of such things during her "tests," only afterward, her sweetest reward.

To her surprise, his forehead creased in a frown. "There's the danger. Because a 'good girl' is told she can only feel sexual pleasure in order to please the man she loves. A woman of profound physical appetite like you deserves more. Tonight you will get exactly what you deserve."

Again he smiled and traced the lacy edge of her bra with his fingertip. Her belly twisted, a tantalizing knot of desire entwined with fear.

"You see, my dear, I've invited a friend over, a successful and very attractive man who knows women and enjoys nothing more than giving them pleasure."

Her throat was suddenly desert-dry.

He stroked her hair again, the protective gesture belying his provocative words. "Your test tonight is this: to make love to my friend, here on this bed. Then, when he's buried deep inside you, I'd like you to come on his cock. Loudly. Don't hold back, because I'll be listening from the other room."

"I can't do that. I can't cheat on you." Yet in spite of her protest, she was already very wet *down there*.

He snorted softly. "Is it cheating if you do it with my blessing?"

"You know I've never come for real with another man."

He narrowed his eyes. "Which reminds me, I want you to promise that you will not fake your orgasm with him tonight. We don't want you to fall back into your bad habits, do we?"

"No, Sir, but..."

"There then, it's settled."

Her body trembled faintly—whether with terror or excitement she wasn't sure. "Please, I... I'm not sure I can let go with somcone else."

His face softened. "Dear Laura, have I ever given you a challenge, no matter how difficult, that you haven't ended up enjoying very much?"

"No, Sir," she admitted.

"Just remember that this 'test' is really about your owning your power. Use him in any way you like to meet your goal—he's most willing to help you succeed. Come, come, what's with the pout?"

"I'm sorry, Sir, I still don't understand why you want this. It feels wrong."

"On the contrary, it's absolutely the right thing to do. If I'm the only man you ever climax with, then you'll always wonder, deep in your heart, if you could do it with another lover. I want you to know this power exists within you. Only then will I be sure you have chosen to serve *me* and are not just swept up in a romantic fantasy designed to brainwash women into ignorance of their own potential."

He was so reassuring—like a kindly schoolmaster or a caring therapist—that she couldn't quite believe he was serious. It was true that she had occasionally wondered if her new responsiveness could translate to sex with another man.

"But, Sir...aren't you worried I might like him better?"

Her sauciness brought a smile. "Excellent point. *My* test is to trust you won't prefer greener pastures. So if—I mean 'when'—you pass, we'll both have cause to celebrate. Just the two of us." His eyebrows lifted in promise. "Will you try your best for me?"

What else could she say but "Yes, Sir"?

"Good girl. He's here already actually. We've been relaxing over a drink and a very interesting video in my study. But first I want to give you a few moments alone to prepare yourself for what is to come." He bent over and kissed her on the forehead.

"Good luck."

With a final squeeze of her shoulder, he rose and disappeared into the hallway.

He was just pretending of course. Trying to get her all excited with the forbiddenness of it. Damn if it wasn't working, too. Her heart was hammering in her chest, and her thighs were slippery with her juices. She took a slow breath to calm herself, but that only made matters worse. Her belly filled with a prickling sensation, lifting her up and up, almost as if she were about to have an orgasm on the spot. Would it count if she came now? Just by thinking about the "exam"?

He simply couldn't be serious. But then again, his other tests had always gone exactly as described, once he'd pushed her past her inhibitions. She never dreamed she was capable of the things he "made" her do. Her first assignment was to watch them make love in the mirrored door of his closet with all the lights on. She saw her own face blush scarlet with shyness, yet from the start she was secretly thrilled by the sight of their bodies joined in that timeless dance. He then cajoled her into masturbating for him—first discreetly in bed, then sitting, legs splayed, on a chair before him so he could see better. At last he convinced her to perform for his video camera, fingers clawing at her clit while she plowed herself with a fat, lifelike dildo, because he said he wanted to study her unique rhythms and techniques during the lonely times when they were apart.

Confident he'd turned her into an unregenerate exhibitionist, he challenged her to take on "backdoor love," not just to submit to it, but to enjoy it so much she'd beg for it. Step by step he orchestrated her anal sensual awakening until she regularly initiated their evening's lovemaking by kneeling before him with a well-used tube of lube in her outstretched hands, imploring,

"Please fuck me deep in the ass tonight, Sir. Punish me for being such a horny slut."

Naturally, none of this would have happened if it hadn't been for their first time as lovers. Their first few dates had been magic, but she'd kept things chaste—for fear she would ruin the wonderful chemistry. On that special night she somehow let him kiss and kiss her into an erotic stupor, but as he was leading her to his bedroom, the confession slipped from her lips: *I don't come. With other people, I mean. I enjoy it, but I don't come. Just so you know.*

The look on his face—well, he didn't insult her with pity. It was understanding mixed with a glimmer of challenge. He said, "Tonight I'll make sure you enjoy yourself very much."

Slow and patient, he caressed and kissed her, savoring every inch of her skin until her body seemed to melt into the sheets.

"We can do *it* now," she finally whispered.

"No, I like this. I'm going to touch you this way all night."

"Don't you want to come?" She pressed her hand against his hard-on, still cloaked in his trousers.

He pulled away. "I won't come until you do."

"That might be never," she laughed.

"So be it."

His gallant refusal had a surprising effect. No other man had ever cared enough about her to put her pleasure before his own. Oddly, by putting himself in her place, he freed her. A few minutes later she did come, her cunt twitching and drooling all over his soft lips and fluttering tongue. Her release was so profound, in that moment she became his.

In the days since, he'd shown her he knew just how to treat a treasured possession. But could that mean giving it away?

* * *

A male form filled the lighted rectangle of doorway. She sucked in her breath.

It was only the Master, holding something shiny in his hand.

"We've decided it will be easier if we blindfold you," he said, holding out a satin sleep mask.

She exhaled quietly. So it *was* just a mind game. While blindfolded she could pretend she was giving herself to another man, when it was really the Master "testing" her. She would play it perfectly, too, never letting on until the scene was over.

In the new, deeper darkness, she felt his warmth recede. She smiled.

He drew near again.

Every muscle in her body stiffened.

This was not the Master. She could feel it. Smell it. The faint scent of aftershave, whisky, unfamiliar male spice.

"Laura?"

Now she could hear it, too, a stranger's voice, slightly higher in pitch, but melodious and assured.

"Yes...Sir?" she croaked.

"I don't mean to be rude, but he'd rather I not give you my name. Please call me 'Professor,' since I'll be administering your exam." His voice was silky with amusement.

A man with a sense of humor. That was good. Still, she was finding it difficult to breathe.

"First I want to make it clear that you are totally in charge here. Please feel free to tell me exactly what to do. I won't let a bit of reserve on your part stop me, but of course I will immediately respect the safewords—'cancel the final' was it?"

"All right...Professor." Her own voice sounded so agreeable. Could it be this simple to slide from virtue to sluthood by any definition of the word?

He laughed amiably. "Usually I like to take my time courting a beautiful lady. So I was thinking that a nice back massage might be a good way to get to know each other. Would that be amenable to you?"

"I suppose so, Professor."

"Excellent. Then if you would take off your robe and turn over on your stomach?"

The cool air on her back made her realize her whole body was moist with anticipation.

"May I unhook your brassiere? I wouldn't want to get massage oil on it."

"Yes, of course, Professor."

With an expert click of his fingers, the bra fell open. They hadn't met a minute ago and already she was allowing him to undress her.

His hands were large, strong, hot. Her muscles gradually relaxed under the flowing, oiled strokes. All the while he spoke to her in a soothing voice—about a Swedish massage course he'd taken in college and different styles of massages he'd experienced in his international business travels. Japanese shiatsu, Thai, hot stone.

"May I go farther down now?"

"Y-yes, Professor."

Now he turned his manual skills to her lower back, dipping down to knead her buttocks rhythmically. In spite of herself she moaned. Loud enough for the Master to hear.

"You're all flushed and pink now. So beautiful. Could you turn on your back now, please? We mustn't neglect the other half."

Dizzy with pleasure, she obeyed.

"We won't be needing this anymore, will we?" He pulled the bra straps down over her arms.

She fought the urge to cover her breasts.

"My god, you are a lovely, lovely girl. May I...kiss them?"

Blind as she was, she could feel his gaze warming her bare flesh. Her faithless nipples stood up high and hard. She nodded assent.

Wet heat encircled her left nipple, while the right received gentle flicks of a large, knowing thumb.

"Oh Jesus," she groaned.

He kissed and fondled her there until she squirmed, helplessly aware that the skimpy thong had done nothing to stop her juices from pooling on the sheet beneath her ass. But only the tiniest part of her cared about such things any longer. Why not surrender to these delicious sensations, so pure, permitted yet sinfully sweet? The Master wanted her to do this. She was serving *him* by letting this courtly stranger have his way with her.

If only the guy weren't so god dammed slow about it.

At long last his fingers crept down over her belly, resting over her mons. "May I?"

"Yes, Professor, please, yes."

He pressed his hand over the small lace triangle covering her groin.

She whimpered.

"I'm in a quandary. Perhaps you can help me?" His voice was thicker now, but still admirably composed. "Shall we keep these pretty panties on? I know you like to masturbate through your underwear to warm up."

Her eyes shot open under the blindfold. "What are you talking about?"

"Your Master showed me that delightfully naughty video of you pleasuring yourself. And the first thing you did was this." He pushed the lace deeper into the groove of her slit, in truth exactly the way she liked to do it when she was in the mood for self-love.

Instinctively her legs dropped open. His finger continued its subtle but very effective assault on her swollen clitoris.

She hissed her pleasure, tilting her hips up to increase the pressure. Shame mixed with pleasure pushed her ever closer to surrender. The Master had let this stranger see her perform a woman's most private act, an obscene show she'd meant for the eyes of her one true love alone. No wonder this man was so good, rubbing her clit just so. The Master had trained him to please her. Her pussy was positively weeping now, and a new worry assailed her. She was supposed to come on his cock, not his fingers.

"Why don't I rub you through your panties until you ask me to take them off?" the Professor suggested teasingly.

"Now," she choked. "Take them off now."

"What a fine idea."

She brought her legs together so he could slip the thong over her hips. As he gently parted her thighs again, the scent of her excitement flooded her nostrils.

"Oh my, just like the video. Such a pretty pussy, so swollen and wet. You're gorgeous, simply gorgeous." He resumed his ministrations, one hand holding open her outer lips, while the other strummed skillfully.

God, this was easy, too easy. The Master knew it would be, didn't he? He'd always known she was a sex-crazed slut who craved the chance to prove how truly depraved she was, test by test. This time she would prove him right again by coming on this faceless man's cock.

"Take off your clothes and put on a condom," she barked out.

"A very eager student indeed," he laughed, but obligingly got up from the bed. She heard the scrape of a zipper, the rustle of clothes hitting the carpet.

"Let me feel it first, before you put the condom on." She reached toward him.

He took her hand and guided it to his cock. The shaft was thick, though not as sturdy as the Master's, but it seemed longer, curving upward like a satiny stalk.

She gave him a squeeze. "I like it."

"It likes you," he breathed.

Before he'd just been a pair of hands, warm lips, a voice, but she was thrilled that this stranger was as turned on by the game as she was. He stretched out on the bed beside her. Groping her way in her darkness, she straddled him, gripped the rubber-sheathed head of his penis and eased him inside.

He groaned and pushed himself all the way in.

She paused, drinking in the new sensations. The unfamiliar girth of his cock, the slightly narrower hips, the scent of male arousal through the aftershave—sandalwood, cumin and cloves.

"Show me what you can do, Laura," he urged. "Remember, you're getting a grade on it."

Was he taunting her? She'd always done well on exams, and by god, she'd show him just how good she was. She began sliding up and down his shaft, ever so slowly, grinding her clit against his belly on the downstroke. She was doing just what the Master said, using him for her pleasure.

"Play with my breasts," she ordered.

He leaned up and took a nipple in his mouth, tweaking the other between his fingers. His free hand crept around to her buttock, slapping her lightly in encouragement. Then, to her surprise, his finger dipped into her tender crevice.

"No," she cried. This desire was too private to share with a stranger.

Undaunted, he tightened his grip, his finger still buried in her crack. "Your Master told me you like this. He told me the best way to make you come is to diddle your asshole like a clit. Wasn't he telling the truth?"

She was too flustered to reply. Of course the Master never lied.

He began to tease her sensitive back hole in earnest. Her answer was to writhe and groan at the searing pleasure. This was the Master's signal for her to climax when she was on top. He'd obviously educated this man in every secret, every trick to her sexual response. It was as if he were here in the room with them purring his instructions.

Now her examiner tapped her asshole like a little drum as if to say: *Come, Laura, come.*

But suddenly she wasn't sure she could take the ultimate step. "I'm not sure I can finish with you inside," she whimpered.

"Listen to me," came a low growl in her ear. "If you pass this test, you'll get your ass fucked good. To *punish* you for being such a *horny slut.*"

She gasped. These were the very words the Master used to trigger her orgasm. In the next instant, her well-schooled cunt spasmed obediently around the foreign cock lodged deep inside her. A fireball ripped through her belly, bursting in stars of psychedelic light behind her eyelids. She bellowed like an animal, her cries tearing her throat raw.

No doubt the Master heard her, and very likely the rest of the neighborhood as well.

The Professor began to pound up into her, moaning with abandon. She gripped him between her legs, reveling in her achievement. Just as the Master promised, she had passed his final exam with flying colors.

Afterward, her temporary lover pulled her close, whispering

words of praise for her fine performance. She gave him an affectionate kiss on the cheek, for she was thankful for his willingness to please her. But her deepest gratitude was reserved for the man in the next room. How had he known this unimaginable transgression would make her feel closer to him than ever before and all the more desperate to have him reclaim her—mouth, cunt and ass?

He was truly her Master, and she his most fortunate slave.

She smiled into the darkness, knowing the celebration had only just begun.

BRIDLE PARTY

Teresa Noelle Roberts

Myra's eyes grew wide as she took in the scene around her. She and her Master, Zan, had been to the Petersons' before, for a Fourth of July picnic, but on this occasion their friends' small hobby farm had been transformed into a strange erotic tableau. Even though Myra had known they were coming to a BDSM event today, she'd had no idea what to expect. Zan liked to surprise her sometimes, and all he'd said was to bring sunscreen and wear comfortable, casual clothes and sneakers. She'd been mystified but eager, anticipating something along the lines of exhibitionistic bondage out among the fruit trees. But the scene that greeted them was unexpected.

Powerfully erotic, charming as a twisted version of a childhood game—and for her, intimidating.

"Pony play?" she whispered. "I didn't know you were into pony play."

Zan put his arm around her shoulder. "I don't know if I am, but it seemed worth checking out when I heard Julie and

Bob were hosting an event. The tack's sexy as hell, and you'll look great in it." His voice took on a darker, richer, more menacing quality as he added, "and I love the idea of training you. Controlling you with just a word and a touch of the reins. Guiding you through a course with a dressage whip or a crop. Making you into a well-trained little animal who'll perform at my command."

She gulped. Zan had hit on a word bound to alarm her: *perform*. And damn him, he knew, though he didn't know she was really nervous, not just roller-coaster scared. He flashed an evilly sexy smile at her and put one firm hand on the back of her neck, making her knees even weaker than they already were.

At least this was the good kind of weak in the knees. Her nipples perked and her cunt clenched at the sudden, claiming gesture.

"For now, observe. Decide what you think looks like fun. Then I'll tell you what you're actually trying, slave."

Damn him. Zan's words—no, just his voice—went straight to her cunt. Straight to her will. Myra wanted to rebel, wanted to say she couldn't possibly do this, but when he addressed her in that tone—when he called her *slave* that way, hotly and possessively—she knew she'd have a hard time saying no.

Not because she feared punishment. Zan rarely punished her. But because she wanted to obey, wanted to make Zan happy. Even if the setup frightened her.

Following his command, she studied the scene around her. A dozen "ponies" were gathered in a makeshift paddock delineated by ribbon and tomato stakes. Most were in shorts and T-shirts with a bridle and perhaps a tail pinned onto the shorts, but a few of the ponies were in full tack: boots with hooves, headpieces with ears and manes, and leather harnesses with attached tails. Since it was a warm early summer day and the farm was private, some wore very little else, treating the spectators to views of breasts and buttocks. Not all of them were muscular, conventionally hot people who Myra would have expected to look good in a few leather straps and a tail, but somehow they all looked sexy. Freed of constraint, Myra thought, because they'd taken on the unself-conscious grace of the animals they were pretending to be. One was eating an apple from the hand of someone who reached over the almost imaginary fence. A few were cantering around like real horses working off excess energy, and a man and woman were quietly nuzzling each other. None of the ponies, as far as Myra could tell from a distance, were speaking. That didn't look bad at all. A little silly, but fun, like playing make-believe as a kid. She could handle playful and silly.

As she watched, a dom led a pony girl out of the paddock, using reins he'd just attached to her bridle. She stepped high, half prancing horse, half dancer. Her eyes shone and her cheeks were rosy with excitement. She was one of the ones in full gear, which meant she wore very little except strapping harnesses, adorable ears and high boots—not even underwear—and it suited her lithe, muscular body. All her movements were graceful and precise, perfect—as if they had been choreographed, as the dom led her to a real paddock where a few other ponies and Masters were.

And where most of the spectators were gathered.

Secondhand panic struck as Myra saw the curious, avid faces of the others who watched the pony girl's precise, practiced movement. She glanced down, not wanting to be part of that gawking mob, not wanting to add to the woman's discomfort, although Myra had no reason to think she was feeling any. In fact, the pony looked like she was having a great time, and a small smile was apparent on her face as she pranced under direction. But seeing that show, and the avid, curious or just lustful faces of the people watching, Myra wanted to run away. Myra knew what Zan wanted, though, and she wanted to please him more than she wanted to give in to her old fears, so she stepped closer and joined the crowd. Zan stood behind her, arms around her. As soon as he pulled her close to his hard body, Myra let out a breath she hadn't known she was holding and was able to really see, not just react.

It wasn't a crowd, not really. Maybe fifteen or twenty people, and some of them were ponies waiting their turn in the ring. But they were still an audience. Still watching and judging, even though those with pony gear on were doing their best to pretend they were just horses, and so only minimally interested.

And yet the pony girls and boys looked like they were having a great time. Performing for an audience, yes, but also having fun. Men and a few women in pony gear pulled carts or were ridden by leather-clad dominants. Julie Peterson, dressed in a steampunk-styled dark green riding habit, was in one of the carts, being pulled by Bob. The usually intense lawyer looked more content and relaxed pulling a cart, while wearing ears and a tail and sporting a harness rig and bridle, than he looked in his normal clothes; he adeptly followed the silent commands Julie gave with her reins. Two women in elaborately plumed and maned headpieces with bridles and blinders, beautiful hoof boots and matching harness rigs did what appeared to be dressage under the direction of a man who smiled like a kid with the best toys in the world as he worked with them. The woman Myra had seen escorted from the paddock began working through a similar routine with her owner. Beyond the paddock, several ponies appeared to be racing through the orchard; at least they were running and people in regular clothes were urging them on.

Watching them perform.

"I want to do this for you," Myra said to Zan, "but I don't know if I can. They're all having so much fun, and it's so sexy looking. And I want to try it—if only so I can prance around in a little leather harness, tail and those adorable ears, with you telling me what to do. But it's going to be hard for me with all these people watching. What if I screw up completely?"

Zan pulled her even closer, his grip both possessive and tender, soothing and arousing. "No one expects you to do it perfectly the first time. At least I hope not, because I don't know what I'm doing either and I'm pretty sure it takes teamwork to look as good as Bob and Julie or the women doing dressage." She heard his smile although she couldn't see it. "And I'm not even going to try to ride you. My feet would drag on the ground."

"That's a relief, anyway." She schooled her muscles to relax, trying to remember all the techniques she'd learned to overcome stage fright—techniques that hadn't helped when she really needed them. She felt her body softening, arousal and curiosity starting to overcome instinctive panic.

But Zan knew her too well. "What's really bothering you? You take a couple of dance classes every week. This should be easy to pick up."

She tugged on his shirt, a signal for "need to talk in private." Zan led her away from the cavorting ponies and proud owners to a quiet place by the vegetable garden. There, surveyed only by a few chickens inside a fence, Myra could articulate. "I take dance classes, but I don't perform. And you know why? I can't stand the audience staring at me. That's how I flubbed my audition to Walnut Hill when I was a kid."

"The performing arts school?"

She nodded. "I was a serious ballet student as a kid. Danced in the Boston *Nutcracker* starting when I was eight. When I was thirteen, I got contacts and everything changed. I'd always taken my glasses off when I performed; I could see well enough to keep track of my blocking, but the audience was a blur. The Walnut Hill audition was the first time I wore contacts onstage and I could make eye contact with people in the audience. I could see their faces as they weighed my abilities. I froze, forgot my choreography and ran off the stage in tears. I don't think my teacher from those days has forgiven me yet. I know my mother still hasn't."

She'd been doing her best to address her words to the chickens, not wanting to look into Zan's face as she confessed the twenty-year-old trauma that stood between her adult self and the obedience she yearned to give him. He moved then, so she couldn't avoid his eyes, and put his big hands on her shoulders. "I will. My good slave doesn't always have to succeed as long as she's willing to try. And you'll try this, Myra. If it's too much, use your safeword. We'll stop and that's fine. But you *will* try. Remember, no one else really matters. They're just noise. You have an audience of one—me—and I'll always appreciate you. So you'll do this."

Hot moisture flooded both Myra's eyes and her cunt. He understood she wanted to give him this, but needed the order and the affirmation so she could get past the panic. The ponies looked like they were having so much fun, and the doms did too. They were enjoying the playful, fun-loving aspect as much as the ponies were and also, she suspected, reveling in the control—in showing off how well trained and obedient their ponies were. She wanted to be part of it, almost as much as she wanted to obey Zan.

Zan brushed away her tears with a big, gentle finger.

He slipped his other hand inside the waistband of her shorts, infiltrating her panties. She gasped at the invasion, at the pleasure that seared her as he brushed over her clit and glided between her slick cunt lips. "Just as I thought." She squirmed against his questing, teasing fingers as her arousal spiraled out of control. "You needed the order, didn't you? Needed me to push you."

"I couldn't...on my own. But I'll obey you, even when it scares me. Maybe especially when it scares me." Pleasure built, obliterating the fear, or at least putting it in perspective. She belonged to Zan, and she'd take risks to obey him that she wouldn't take on her own. And in return, he gave her this freedom to rise above her limitations, to be braver.

To be a pony, if it pleased him. Even if people were watching.

She pictured herself following Zan's silent commands conveyed through reins and gestures, creating a dance with him the way the ponies and owners she'd been watching did.

And the orgasm burst from her. Her cry of "Yes, Master, yes!" burst out loud enough to startle the chickens into clucking indignation.

"Good girl," Zan crooned, holding her close, hard against her. "Good, brave girl."

When she came back to herself, her Master said, "I'm going to talk to Julie. She might have ideas about helping you through the scary part."

Which was how Myra found herself in a quiet part of the back forty, with no one there but Julie, Ben and of course Zan. Julie had scrounged loaner gear from a few people, so Myra wore a leather strapping harness in a fetching shade of dark green. The harness was over her T-shirt and yoga pants because it didn't fit quite right and would rub uncomfortably. Her Nikes didn't add to the overall stylish effect, either, but feeling the tail swish against her legs, experiencing the weight of the bridle and headpiece, made her feel sexy as sin even if she wasn't as fashionable as some of the other ponies. Her faux tail was chestnut brown, although the ears on the headpiece, borrowed from someone else, were black. That didn't matter to Myra. She couldn't see the ears, but she knew they were there.

She pranced in place experimentally while Zan and Julie conferred, trying to imitate the cantering high step she'd seen on other ponies. It felt good, natural, but she gave herself permission to misstep occasionally. It was like learning a new style of dance.

Only much sexier.

And much more nerve-wracking. Despite the safe location, mostly hidden from prying eyes, Myra was keyed up from anxiety as much as arousal, and she kept scanning the tree line for new arrivals.

Zan and Julie finished talking and came to her, each carrying another piece of gear. "Open your mouth," Zan said, and slipped in a simple plastic bit, which he attached to the bridle.

The bridle, effectively gagging her, also slowed the frantic what-ifs that had been racing through her mind, as if the temporary loss of her human voice removed some of the words storming her brain. Some of the bad tension left her body, replaced by desire.

Then Julie stepped up. "I have a surprise for you, pretty girl," she said softly and soothingly, as if speaking to an actual flighty horse. "Something to put Zan's nervous pony a little more at ease." She held up two small leather objects, but it wasn't until she began to attach one to Myra's bridle that Myra realized what they were.

Blinders.

As Myra blinked, trying to get used to her suddenly narrowed vision, Julie moved to the side and effectively disappeared.

As would anyone who might be watching who wasn't directly in front of her.

Myra caught just a glimpse of Zan as he moved behind her and took up the reins. "Eyes front," he ordered. "Follow the reins."

He slapped at her gently with the reins and clicked his tongue, which she guessed was a signal to move. She stepped forward, hesitantly at first, then working up to a high-stepping prance.

She could do this. With her Master behind her, it didn't matter who else might be around.

Especially if she couldn't see.

THE RED ENVELOPE

Erzabet Bishop

H appy birthday!" Jen hugged me as we bustled inside the coffee shop to meet for our weekly gossip session. It was starting to rain, and my hair was becoming a mass of wild red tangles. Jen, beautiful as always, looked like she had stepped out of a magazine, with her long black tresses and exotic features. I was struck by our differences and tried not to let my ever-present voluptuousness drag me down. Her sensuous curves never failed to stir longings in my heart that I quickly squashed down. Not to mention the moisture that began to dampen my panties. I had read one too many bondage novels apparently. I could imagine her mouth doing wicked things to my breasts and investigating regions of my body that hadn't been touched in years. *Oh, inner voice, you really, really need to be quiet.*

Standing in line, I eyed the pastry case with feigned disinterest as images of lemon-glazed pound cake danced across my imaginary taste buds. I had been so good. Not a crumb in months. It was my birthday damn it. *Willpower.* Yes. Nothing tastes as good as being thin feels. *Ugh*. Except maybe just one little cake pop. I bit my lip and tried to rein in the carb monster in me that had a sweet tooth big enough to swallow Manhattan.

"So, do you have anything planned for your big night?" Jen waggled her eyebrows at me suggestively and I had to stifle a very unladylike snort. Woefully tearing my attention away from the display of cupcakes and muffins, I pulled out my latest smut novel and grinned.

"Yes. It just so happens that one of my favorite authors has a new book out and I decided to treat myself this afternoon. I can hardly wait to get home, open a bottle of wine and settle down in a nice pair of sweats for a smoking hot night of sexy bondage." I laughed and tucked the book back in my purse, trying not to laugh at the shocked face of the older woman that stood behind me in line. Good grief. *I just want some fun. Is that too much to ask?*

We approached the counter and ordered.

"Oh no you don't. My treat." Jen booted me out of the way and paid.

Waiting for our drinks at the end of the bar, I longingly caressed the dessert case with my eyes once more before relegating myself to the skinny mocha, no whip that was set on the counter in front of me. *Sigh*. I have the willpower to resist. No blowing the whole day's points just for one blissful bite of cupcake. Or three. Inside, I sniffled just a little. Too much temptation everywhere.

"Come on, girl. Let's find a table." Jen hustled her way through the crowded coffeehouse and found a spot in an isolated corner.

I sat down, relieved to be off my feet. It had been a long day and my heels were making themselves known.

Jen sank down in her chair and dropped her purse onto the

table. Opening the flap, she withdrew a red envelope and slid it toward me.

"Happy birthday!" A mischievous look twinkled in her eyes.

"What is it? Some kind of birthday-card porn to make me forget my diet and keep me from drooling over the lemon pound cake I'm missing out on?" I snarked, snatching up the card.

"No smartass. It's your birthday present." Jen took a sip of her latte, eyes fixed on me over the rim of her cup as she drank.

"Okay." I pouted. Darn. Jamming the key to my apartment in the corner of the envelope, I ripped it open.

It was an invitation. At first I was unsure what I was reading. I looked up, questioning her with my eyes.

"Go on." Jen nodded. "Read it."

The Phoenix Club Proudly Presents:
The Red Envelope Auction Event
Surrender to your deepest fantasies and
meet the Dom/Domme of your dreams. Enter the
auction and find your true Master or Mistress.
10:00 a.m. Saturday
until sundown Sunday evening.
A weekend of sexual dominance and submission.
Invitation required for entry.

"Are you out of your mind?" I stood up and the table wobbled, almost spilling what was left of our drinks.

"No." Jen stared me down and pointed to the chair. *"Sit. Down. Now."*

I growled and plopped back down in the chair.

"What the hell is this?" I hissed, waving the envelope in her face.

"It's an invitation to the club I go to on occasion and being the awesome friend that I am, I thought you might want to come and check it out." She pointed to the book jutting from my purse and the smutty bondage girl draped across the glossy cover. "You are always telling me how much you like reading about kink." She grabbed my hand and I tried to tamp down the shock. "You are a natural for the lifestyle. I love you, Olivia. You are my best friend. You have been working so hard to shed the weight your doctor wants you to lose that you haven't let yourself breathe. At all. For months now I have stood by and marveled at your will. I can't believe you've lost thirty-five pounds. That is so amazing. *But you never have fun.*" Jen shook her head and tears made her eyes overbright.

"Jen, I..." Tears welled up in my own eyes and I struggled to blink them away. There were too many emotions raging through my mind and I was on overload.

"No. There is no refusal. This is something you have needed forever." She gave me a stern smile. " You *are* beautiful, honey." She stared me down and I nodded, the lump lodged in my throat feeling suddenly like a large golf ball. I was going to a bondage party. *Oh. My. God.*

"Come on Olivia! Get out of the damn car." Jen stood by the passenger-side door, tapping her leather-clad foot. In thigh-high boots with a corset outfit that made my panties wet and my inner green-eyed monster spring to life, she was amazing. I on the other hand was not.

"I'm coming. *Sheesh.*" I grabbed my purse, grumbling under my breath, and tried to quiet the butterflies that were rampaging through my stomach.

The Phoenix Club was some distance out of the city. It was in an older, Colonial-style mansion with impeccable grounds.

Manicured lawns and sculptured gardens were guarded by high
stone walls and a massive iron gate with a guardhouse. Jen
had navigated her way through the maze, while I just sat in the
passenger seat lost in my own thoughts. What was I doing here?
I wasn't a submissive. I just loved reading about them. Besides,
didn't subs have to be little size-four nymphets like Jen? How
long had she been in the lifestyle? There were so many questions
I wanted to ask, but as I climbed out of the car and stood in front
of the manse, it didn't seem the right time for twenty questions,
even though they were streaking through my head like wildfire.

So how long have you been a sub?

How many flogger strokes does it take you to come?

Does it hurt? (insert squeak)

How does a fat girl like me fit into this scene?

Ugh. Never mind. Inner voice, you suck.

"Come *on*. We're going to be late." Jen tapped her watch and
I trudged up the stairs in my slimmest gray skirt, cream blouse
and new black heels.

As we approached, the doors opened and a handsome man
in nothing but a pair of shapely leather pants bid us enter.

"Good morning, Mistress Jen."

Mistress? What the fuck?

Jen turned back and gave me a stare that shut my lips before
they had a chance to open. Well. Wasn't that an interesting
development? My friend wasn't a sub at all. She was a *domme*.
I felt my face flame and as she took my hand and led me to the
check-in desk, I followed blindly along behind her.

"Good morning Giselle." A young blonde woman sitting
behind the desk looked up and her eyes lit up as she saw Jen.

"Good morning, Mistress. How many I serve you?" She
remained seated at her station and laid a pen down on the regis-
tration book in front of her.

"I need to sign Olivia in and have her fitted for today's events. Can you assist me with that?"

"Yes, Mistress. Let me call Sergio to come and collect her for her fitting."

"Thank you, Giselle."

"You are most welcome, Mistress. Please let me know if there is *anything* I can do to serve you this weekend." A fine blush crept across her features as she gazed at Jen with longing.

A fierce pang of jealousy sizzled up my spine as I looked at Jen. I didn't have much time to examine my feelings because a young man clad in leather pants appeared to my right.

Jen nodded to him and turned to me.

"Olivia, go with Sergio and let him show you what to do."

Panic spiked through me as I realized she wasn't staying with me the whole time. It must have shown on my face because she gave me a reassuring smile and ran a hand gently down my cheek.

"Don't worry. Just do what he tells you." Jen kissed me lightly on the cheek and a I felt a pulse of desire flood my pussy.

With that she strode away, hips swinging. Her leather boots made their presence known across the marble floor, and I stared after her with longing. This was going to be quite a weekend.

"Suck it in." Sergio led me down the hallway toward the auction room, and I felt faint from the corset's constrictive enclosure. Looking in the mirror back in the room had been a lesson in itself. Sergio apparently was a makeup artist and master of personal style because when I had looked in the mirror, the voluptuous red-haired creature staring back had shapely curves with breasts that threatened to spill from the cups that held them firmly in place. A short leather skirt lay snug against my hips and ass and every time I took a step, my feet wobbled on the fuck-me heels he had somehow gotten me into. Four-inch heels were not something I was used to, so I trotted down the hall next to the male sub like a pony in a show. Complete with collar and leash, I was made up like a Rubenesque bondage doll.

When I started to growl as my breath hitched from exertion, he gave a yank on the leash and swatted me on the butt.

"What?" I stared at him and he paused, giving me a look that would have been at home with any of the doms in my vast library of smutty BDSM novels.

"Lesson number one, subbie. You are here to take orders and do what you are told. This is an honor. Don't blow it." A shadow of annoyance crossed his face and his eyes focused on mine, forcing them down.

I flinched at the tone of his voice, knowing he was right. I was forgetting my place. Assuming I even knew what that was at this point.

"Sergio?" I chanced a look at him and tried to look contrite.

"What?" His eyes shot me a gentle but firm warning and he tugged on the leash. We started moving toward the door at the end of the hallway where others had already gathered, subs on leashes being led in by their handlers.

"Thank you." I hobbled along beside him and he stopped and pointed at my shoes.

"First, you are welcome. Second, if you fall in those things, Mistress J will have my head. Take deliberate steps. Short ones. Like this." He made short, smooth, graceful steps and I did my best to copy his movements.

"Okay. Better. Keep working on it." He led me to the back of the line of subs and handlers and we proceeded through the doors.

* * *

"Ladies and gentlemen, may I present this year's crop of submissive and slave candidates for our Red Envelope event." The crowd of leather-clad dominants applauded, and I felt my legs turn to jelly. All around me, subs that seemed to know their cues removed their shoes and knelt in submissive poses. I did the same, kicking off my heels and lowering myself onto my knees. Legs spread as far as the tight skirt would allow, I put my hands behind my back, thrust my breasts out in front of me and lowered my eyes.

"Before you are a colorful array of the best this season has to offer. Let the silent bidding begin! Submissives and slaves, please line up here and walk the circular path. Your handler will greet you when you return for the next portion of our program."

I stood on wobbly legs and made my way down the line with the other submissives. Ten other women and three men made up our group. As we walked, I recognized music from Isadar's new *Red* album and smiled. Piano music calmed my nerves and before I knew it, the crowd faded away and there was Sergio, waiting to take me to the next stop.

"What's next, Sergio?" I whispered as he led me down a hallway and into one of the grand suites. Ceiling to floor, the room was opulence personified and bigger than my entire apartment. Who lived here? My gaze slid over the queen-size bed, and I knew without a doubt it would be heaven on earth to sleep there.

"You are to disrobe and put yourself in the corner. Your Master or Mistress will join you presently."

"Thank you, Sergio."

"You are most welcome, *cara mia*." He shot me a kind smile and eased himself silently back into the hall.

Showtime.

I unclasped the skirt and let it slide to the floor. The corset laces took a moment, but I loosened them and my breasts fell free, exposed to the chill of the air. Shivering in my panties, I slid them down over my hips and ass and let them fall into the pile of discarded clothes. I saw a pillow stationed in the far corner of the room, so I lowered myself onto my knees there and waited.

The door clicked open and my eyes inadvertently rose. Who would be my Master or Mistress? The suspense was making me wet. All of the things I had read about in books flooded through my mind and my pussy clenched in anticipation.

The click of a boot heel on the marble entrance had me lowering my head before I was caught trying to see.

"Stand up, slave." The voice rolled over me like caramel hot chocolate.

I stood and waited for the next command.

"Approach me. Eyes down, breasts out."

It was her boots that caused the rush of moisture to my pussy. Keeping my eyes down, I moved in front of her and stood, a flush creeping up my face.

"Mistress." I whispered. "How may I, um, serve you?"

Her hand reached out and brushed along my cheek in a familiar stroke of affection.

"You look lovely, Olivia."

"Thank you, Mistress." I forgot myself for a moment and raised my eyes to see what I had been longing for. The leather corset encased her breasts so divinely that I reached out my hand before I realized what I had done.

She grabbed my errant fingers with one hand and, with the other, smacked a riding crop against my ass with a single stroke.

"Ouch!" I yowled, rubbing my sore bum with my hand.

"Impertinence. I will not have such a thing in a slave, Olivia."
Mistress J pulled me toward the bed, her boots clicking across
the floor.

"Lie over the edge of the bed. I want that ripe, supple ass
where I can see it, my naughty pet."

I yelped as the crop came down and flicked against the same
spot she had chanced to hit only moments before.

Her fingers ran along the planes of my back and down the
ivory curves of my backside. Another flick of the crop and I was
moaning beneath her hands, pussy gushing with need.

"You have waited for this moment a long time, Olivia. Sit up
and turn to face me."

I did as she asked, conscious of my nakedness. She was still
fully clothed.

"Are you ready to make your deepest fantasies come to life?"
Her voice caressed me, and I had to close my eyes to hide the
tears that suddenly fell free.

"Olivia. This weekend is a test of sorts. I know you long for
a life beyond the pages of a book." She stroked my face again.
"Open your eyes."

I opened my eyes and nodded, afraid of what my voice would
sound like if I spoke.

"Your safeword is *red*. Repeat it so I know you understand."
Her eyes bored into mine.

"Red. I understand."

"Are you ready to begin?"

"Yes, Mistress." My voice was barely a whisper, but she
heard me.

"Good. Stand up and put your hands on the strap at the top
of the bedpost. Do not let go."

She moved behind me and I heard the zipper on her skirt
coming down and the telltale sound of laces and leather. There

were some other sounds that I couldn't place, but I knew well enough not to turn around. This was my fantasy.

"Don't move, little Olivia."

The crop made its way up my backside, and with two flicks she had me panting.

"Open your legs."

I moved them apart as far as I could and still be able to reach the strap. My ass was on fire and the chill of the room made the wetness of my cunt all the more pronounced as the crop connected with my clit.

I moaned, feeling the sting of the crop once again.

"Wider."

"Yes, Mistress." I endeavored to do as she asked.

She moved closer behind me, wrapping her arms around my body. Pinching my right nipple, her finger delved into the hot cleft between my legs. Something poked my back and I felt the bobble of a cock between my asscheeks.

I started against her, and she soothed me with her hands.

"Stay." She pinched my nipple and ran her hand down my body, making me quiver with desire. Her thumb nudged my clit as she guided the head of the cock inside my sopping cunt.

She took control of my body, the softness of her breasts moving against my back and the wispy brush of her mons on mine as the cock plunged deep into my hungry pussy.

"Harder, Mistress. Please!" I moaned, arching my ass into the air.

She tweaked my clit, and I screamed as wave after wave of sensation tore through my body. My skin was electric. Every touch molten fire.

"What do you want, Olivia?"

"I want you to make me come," I panted. "Oh, please!" I howled as her fingers massaged my engorged nub into an orgasm that left me screaming and trembling against the bedpost.

I sagged against her and she removed the dildo and placed it on the bed.

"Up on the bed, little slave. It's time for your oral examination."

As I nestled down between her downy folds, and my lips found the velvet of her inner thighs, I knew I had come home.

"Don't dawdle; lick my slit."

"Yes, Mistress."

I thought of the book in my purse and smiled. Some dreams really do come true.

GREEN'S

Lisette Ashton

H e treats us like slaves," Sarah hissed.

She had whispered the sentiment into her mobile phone but the words echoed around the haberdashery shop as though they had been bellowed through a megaphone.

Monica glanced at Sarah in surprise.

Old Mrs. Higgins closed her eyes and shook her head in dismay.

Green, his eyes unreadable through his dark glasses, regarded Sarah with an expression that was thin-lipped, inscrutable and unsmiling. It was a moment that transformed the mood of the day into something lethargic and heavy with the threat of impending disaster. Each passing minute dragged like slow-motion footage of an inevitable car crash.

Monica's chest was tight with the sense of anticipation.

An eon later the church bell chimed six times to indicate it was the end of the working day. In the stillness of Green's Haberdashery the sound was like the champagne-cork-popping promise of a long-awaited armistice.

Monica took a step back to watch developments. Old Mrs. Higgins reached for her coat. Sarah was rushing to the doorway with unseemly haste.

"Wait!"

Green snapped the single word as Sarah placed her fingers on the door handle.

Sarah was a large girl. Monica had always used the word *cuddly* when describing her. Green had overheard this euphemism once. He had laughed nastily and said, "That's a fuck of a lot of cuddling."

Monica supposed it was an accurate assessment.

"I have to get home, Mr. Green," Sarah said. "It's my brother's birthday and…"

Her voice trailed off as he walked to the shop door.

Absently, he turned the card that said OPEN so that it would have told late customers that Green's Haberdashery was CLOSED. He drew the bolt on the door, effectively locking himself and his staff in the shop.

Monica drew a low, heavy breath.

It was going to be one of those evenings. A tremor of raw excitement rippled through the inner muscles of her sex. She could feel her nipples tightening inside her bra. She felt momentarily dizzy at the prospect of what might happen.

Green employed three members of staff: herself, Sarah and old Mrs. Higgins.

Green, a broad man, his head shaved bald and his eyes constantly hidden behind shaded spectacles, was known to be a strict disciplinarian. He shouted at those beneath him. He browbeat and bullied subordinates into submission. And he considered all of his employees to be subordinates. He had a reputation for being harsh and brutal and Sarah was not the first person to suggest that he treated his employees like slaves. Sarah was simply the first person stupid enough to say it within Green's hearing.

Monica wondered if Sarah had already learned her lesson. Judging by the way she tried to move past Green to get to the shop doorway and make her escape, Sarah clearly had learned no such thing.

"I have to get home, Mr. Green," Sarah said as she reached for the door handle. "It's my brother's birthday and I promised him I'd bake a cake. You have to let me go home now."

Green stepped to one side.

Monica was chilled to see that he wore a smile. It did not bode well for Sarah.

"Step out of that door without my permission and you're unemployed," he said simply.

Sarah stopped and studied him warily.

"Step out of that door and I'll make sure this is your last day working for me. I'll also make sure that no one in this village will employ you ever again. I have the power to do that. Don't think I'm lying."

Sarah had reached out to grab the door handle. Her hand shrank away from it. She studied him uncertainly. Her lower lip trembled as though she was about to start crying.

"Mr. Green!" It was old Mrs. Higgins. She raised her voice in shocked admonishment. "You can't talk to the young girl like that. She's got to bake a cake for her younger brother. She's done her work here this weekend. You should let her go."

Green turned to glance at her.

"Mrs. Higgins," he began carefully. "I thought you knew better than to intercede when I'm disciplining staff members?"

She opened her mouth to speak and then faltered before words could come from her trembling jaw.

"Didn't you learn my rules the last time you spoke up on someone's behalf?"

The old woman blushed. She placed a protective hand over her rear. When she spoke again her voice was softened by contrition. "I was only trying to say that Sarah has plans for this evening and it's not right to keep her past her scheduled hours in the shop."

Green nodded agreement. "That's right. We don't want to keep anyone waiting unnecessarily in the shop, do we? I don't want to be accused of treating people like slaves, do I?"

Sarah blushed.

Monica, watching intently, bit her lower lip. There was something magnificent about watching Green in action. When it came to dominating subordinates she had never seen anyone better. His control over lesser mortals was magnificent. The inner muscles of her sex clenched with greedy approval.

"I said: *we don't want to keep anyone waiting unnecessarily in the shop, do we?*" he repeated. "Are you going to agree with me, Mrs. Higgins?"

She shook her head. "It was an important call," Mrs. Higgins said quickly. She clutched defensively at the pocket at the front of her uniform tabard.

Monica could see the pocket was distended by the shape of a clunky mobile phone. Vaguely, Monica remembered Mrs. Higgins taking a call earlier that day.

"It was an important call that I had to take," Mrs. Higgins insisted. She spoke with the panicked uncertainty of someone trying to convince herself. "It only meant the customer was waiting for a moment longer than necessary."

"The customer was waiting for eight minutes," Green said.

Mrs. Higgins shook her head.

"It wasn't that long."

"I timed it," he said sternly. "And you know the rules. You know what's expected of you."

He went to the cutting table—the space in the shop where he cut lengths of fabric from long rolls. The table was clear of fabric now that the day had ended. All that remained were a pair of dressmaker's shears and a slender three-foot wooden rule. He picked up the rule and sliced it through the air.

It whistled keenly.

In the silence of the shop the sound was like a gasp of disbelief.

Mrs. Higgins placed a hand over the well-padded rear of her skirt. She shook her head with more authority. "Please, no, Mr. Green. My husband will see. He'll want to know—"

"Eight minutes," Green repeated. His soft-spoken words cut through her protest. "That equates to eight stripes from the rule."

"Please," Mrs. Higgins moaned.

Monica envied the woman for her predicament. She could feel the cheeks of her own backside reddening in empathy. Her heartbeat raced as she imagined herself in Mrs. Higgins's position beneath the glower of Green's furrowed brow.

"You can't do this to her," Sarah said abruptly. She stepped between Green and Mrs. Higgins. She had her hands on her ample hips and fixed him with a defiant glare. "It's not right."

Green nodded affable agreement to Sarah.

"You're absolutely correct. It's not right," he said. His smile twisted to a cynical sneer as he added, "but she's going to suffer a lot less than you before the end of this evening. Do you want to say something else to make your punishment worse?"

Sarah shrank beneath his frown. Gingerly, she stepped away.

"Assume the position, Mrs. Higgins," Green called stiffly.

Mrs. Higgins walked hesitantly to the cutting table.

Monica held herself rigid as she watched. She had worked

with old Mrs. Higgins for the best part of a decade. She was
used to seeing the woman being cowed by Green. The experience was never less than exhilarating.

Slowly, glaring at him with vanquished defiance, Mrs.
Higgins raised the rear hem of her skirt. She pulled the fabric
up in twin fistfuls, raising the curtain of the hem to first reveal
the backs of surprisingly shapely legs. They were evenly tanned
and slender.

As always, Monica noted, they were unsheathed by hosiery.

As the hem of the skirt was raised higher, old Mrs. Higgins
uncovered a backside hidden by a pair of huge white knickers.
The brilliant white of the panties seemed shocking in the dark-
ening twilit gloom of Green's Haberdashery.

Sarah made a strangled gasp of surprise.

Monica ignored her and watched as old Mrs. Higgins word-
lessly bent over the cutting table. She kept hold of her raised hem
so that her panty-covered rear remained on view for Green.

"Granny pants?" Green snorted. There was a note of chuck-
ling derision in his tone. "Is this your idea of protecting yourself, Mrs. Higgins? You're wearing nasty granny pants?"

Mrs. Higgins said nothing. Her cheeks burnt bright
crimson.

Monica envied the woman's predicament. If she had been
bold enough to earn such a publicly humiliating punishment, she
too would have chosen to wear granny pants. She clenched her
thighs tight together, crushing the muscles as her sex clutched
and rippled hungrily.

"I can't stripe your backside through granny pants," Green
grumbled. "They're going to have to come off."

"No," Mrs. Higgins protested. "My husband will see."

"If you don't take them off now I'll film this on your mobile
phone and send the footage to your husband," Green growled

with venom. He reached for the front of her tabard and snatched the phone from the pocket.

Monica wondered if he was touching anywhere else while he pulled the phone free. She could imagine his strong hands exploring the pocket of her tabard, pressing against the needy throb of her sex and reminding her of his insistent nearness. The idea came close to weakening her knees with needy lust.

Green came away holding her mobile phone like a trophy. There was a triumphant smile on his lips. "Now take off those damned granny pants."

Mrs. Higgins did as he demanded.

She pulled the huge pants until they slipped downward and pooled at her ankles. With the pants disappearing she exposed a large, round backside. The muscles of her buttocks were taut. Despite the fact that she was known as "old Mrs. Higgins" there wasn't a millimeter of her legs or backside that suggested advanced age. If anything, the neatly shaved pussy lips that Monica could glimpse at the top of the woman's clenched thighs were suggestive of youthfulness. The puckered ring of her anus was so pale Monica thought the woman could have spent her weekends at a salon for those youthful enough to indulge in anal bleaching.

"Eight stripes," Green said coolly. "And you're going to count them for me."

Mrs. Higgins gripped the sides of the cutting table.

Monica could see that the woman was gritting her dentures tightly.

Sarah stood watching with bewildered dismay. Her jaw hung open with obvious disbelief. She shook her head from side to side as though she would be able to wish away the unwanted scenario.

Green slashed the rule across old Mrs. Higgins's rear. It

sang softly through the air and spat loudly as it kissed her rear. Immediately a dull pink line of burning pain blossomed beneath her buttocks.

"One," she panted.

Green's grin tightened. If she could have seen his eyes, Monica knew they would have been shining with satisfaction. She supposed it was enough that she could see the bulge of his arousal pushing at the front of his jeans.

Punishing the staff was the highlight of his working week.

He slashed the rule across Mrs. Higgins's backside for a second time. This blow left a blazing red line just beneath the first. The sound was loud enough to sting Monica's ears. She could hear Sarah whimpering incredulously as she watched the scene being played out before her.

"Two," Mrs. Higgins said.

Green chuckled softly. Without further hesitation he delivered a third blow.

This one was hard enough to make the air snap as the rule soared toward the woman's rear. The smack of uncompromising wood kissing unyielding flesh was loud enough to echo from the walls of the haberdashery shop.

Watching intently, Monica could feel the throb of her clitoris pulsing with excitement. On ragged breath old Mrs. Higgins said, "Three."

"You can't do this to her," Sarah told him. She did not sound confident. The uncertainty in her voice was almost tangible. "This isn't right," she insisted. "It's not pleasant. It's...it's..."

"It's the way I discipline my staff when they step out of line," Green said coolly. He raised the rule and pointed it at Sarah.

She cowered away from him.

"This is only your first week here, Sarah. You're not yet familiar with the way I run this establishment so you can take this as a lesson. I don't tolerate people stealing time from me."

Almost absently he slashed the rule against old Mrs. Higgins's backside.

The old woman sobbed. "Fuh...four."

"I don't tolerate people stealing money from me."

Again, he casually slashed the rule against Mrs. Higgins's rear.

Again the old woman moaned softly. "Fuh...five." She caught the words on hitching breath. It sounded as though she was stifling groans of either dismay or delight. Monica couldn't tell which.

Green did not seem to have noticed. "And I don't tolerate people treating my customers with disrespect."

He delivered another slash. This one was harder than the others. The rule spat loudly as it bit.

Mrs. Higgins wailed.

Monica envied her for the cunt-clenching pleasure she was obviously enduring. She sorely wished she had been in old Mrs. Higgins's place and been forced to suffer Green's wrath.

"Six," Mrs. Higgins managed eventually. She released each sibilant with a shuddering sigh that sounded almost orgasmic.

"You've broken all three of those rules today," Green told Sarah. He raised the rule and pointed it beneath her nose. "If I wasn't such a pushover I'd be throwing your fat backside out of this shop and telling you never to come back." He advanced on her, wielding the rule above his head as though he intended to thrash her where she stood.

"I'm sorry, Mr. Green," she stammered. She seemed to know what had caused the majority of his ire because she said, "I didn't mean to say you treat your staff like slaves. It won't happen again. None of it. I promise. Please don't hit me."

"I'm not paying you for this week," he told her. "Not after

all you've stolen from me."

"I understand," she sobbed miserably.

"I ought to thrash your bare backside until the stripes are tattooed there forever."

Sarah moaned. She clutched a hand against her rear.

"You'll come in here one hour early on Monday morning and clean this shop to compensate me for stealing time and money."

"Yes, Mr. Green," she trembled.

"You'll stay for one hour extra each night to clean up at the end of the day."

"Yes, Mr. Green,"

"And you're going to bend over backward to help every customer in here from now on, or so help me I'll have you bent forward over the cutting table at the end of the day so you can feel the sting of this rule."

To illustrate his point he slammed the rule against Mrs. Higgins's backside.

The old woman cried out in surprise.

Monica could detect a note of raw arousal in her groan. She empathized. She was ready to release her own roar of sexually tortured excitement.

"Get out of here now," Green told Sarah. "But be prepared to come back in here on Monday morning with a drastically improved attitude."

He had barely finished speaking when the bell rang to indicate that Sarah had shot the bolt and fled the shop.

Old Mrs. Higgins pulled herself away from the cutting table and began to pull her pants back up. She let her skirt fall back over her striped rear and said, "You do that too well. I am so wet right now I'm going to spend the entire weekend fucking my husband senseless."

"You're welcome, Mrs. Higgins," Green said. He gave her back her phone and said, "I've caught a couple of shots on there that Bill might enjoy seeing." He turned his cheek so she could grace him with a kiss to show her gratitude.

"Does your wife know how lucky she is to have such a gifted husband?" Mrs. Higgins asked.

Green glanced at Monica. "Well, Mrs. Green?" he asked. "Do you know how lucky you are?"

Monica sniffed with mock disdain. She strutted confidently over to him and clutched the bulge at the front of his pants. "None of us are lucky in this shop," she said purposefully. "The owner treats us all like slaves."

BREAKING
FIONA

Cecilia Duvalle

F iona walked around the block three times. With each circuit, she paused in front of Malcolm's building before continuing. The doorman nodded in greeting each time she passed, and as she neared him on her fourth pass, he opened the door for her and cocked his head, directing her inside. Of course he had recognized her, and the gentle upward tilt of his lips showed a sense of empathy though she doubted he had any idea what was going through her mind. She didn't think Malcolm made a habit of sharing his extensively kinky life with the doorman. How many times had she slipped through this door on her way to visit him without even looking at the man who so kindly helped her out of the endless loop she had been forcing on herself?

She paused as she passed him and caught his eye.

"Thanks."

He tilted his head and tipped his cap at her. "Have a nice evening, Ms. Swenson."

She smiled back but didn't have anything else to say to him.

That he even knew her name surprised her. She spent the short elevator ride staring at the DOWN button. How had she gotten herself into this?

Malcolm answered the door with a broad gesture, inviting her in. The formality of it made her giggle. Maybe he was feeling a little discomfited by this whole thing as well.

"You're late. How many times did you walk around the block?"

She brushed past him and unbuttoned her overcoat.

"You were watching me?"

"Nope. Just know you. Nervous?"

She tossed her coat on the chair closest to the door and crossed her arms.

"Nervous? Oh...I don't know if I'm nervous so much as pissed at myself for getting into this. I should know better than to play drinking games with you."

Malcolm was looking her over. She had come dressed as he had ordered her to. Once she gave her word on something, drunk or not, she carried through. He reached out and took her by the wrists to reposition her arms so they were at her side. She shifted her weight, and he slid his hands along her hips to straighten her out again, leading her body as naturally as a dancer.

"You sure you want to go through with this?" His voice was kind and firm—the voice he used with his subs. He was circling. Inspecting. She wore nothing but her underwear and a bra under her coat. The trip over to his apartment from hers had been an exercise in circumnavigating vents along the way.

"I am not going back on the bet, if that's what you mean."

"You can be so fucking stubborn, Fiona. I just want to hear your consent, and then we'll get started."

She knew Malcolm just as well as she knew anyone. They

dated for two weeks before they realized they wouldn't make a great long-term team. She wasn't attracted to him, either. He was much too small for her taste. She preferred men over six feet tall who, when they submitted to her, made her feel like a goddess. The power of controlling huge muscles, keeping them at bay and testing their limits was her mainstay. Malcolm was her same height, and when she wore heels, she towered over him. She wouldn't get any enjoyment out of domming him if she tried. They'd been friends for years, teamed up to play with a few subs, but never this. When they hung out, they spent hours coming up with creative new mind fucks to use on their subs. She knew him well enough to trust him completely. And, she was sure that he knew her well enough to fuck with her in ways no one else could ever dream.

"I give consent to you, Malcolm...for this evening, I will..." She paused and took a deep breath before uttering words she thought she would never say. "I will submit to you."

They'd already hammered out the details earlier in the week via email and text, a long list of DO's and DON'Ts and how the bet would be considered paid.

Malcolm put his palms against her upper arms and moved them up and down, warming up her skin. He kissed her forehead and smiled.

"You're scared shitless."

He wasn't quite right. It was more that she knew what he was capable of, and she knew what she would have done to him if he had lost the bet.

She laughed. "No, I just know you...and...okay. Maybe a little."

He pulled her into an embrace and she softened against him. He held her like that for a while before breaking the contact and steering her toward his spare room where he kept all his equipment. He had set up his massage table in the center of the room, and his cross was off to the side. A neat coil of purple hemp rope, a long leather flogger, a blindfold and a ball gag sat on the counter in preparation.

Her heart rate increased at the sight of the ball gag, an instant panic that she had not expected. She spun around, ready to leave.

"No gags. I was pretty clear about that." She saw from the expression on his face that she had been caught up in one of his simplest mind fucks. "Shit...Malcolm!" She reached out and hit him in the arm. "That was seriously not funny."

He picked up the ball gag and dangled it in front of her to tease her like someone might use a plastic spider to tease an arachnophobe. She pushed it away from her, and he laughed. But he was watching her with that serious look he used with his subs. Fuck. She was screwed.

"I'm serious, Malcolm. You know how I feel about that." She pulled out her domme voice, commanding and demanding respect. "Bets are off..."

She pushed past him. He followed her out of the room and grabbed her. He tossed the gag on the sofa in the living room and held her until the adrenaline shakes dissipated. He stroked her and cooed in his sweet baritone that she had never been close enough to hear. It was warm and kind. Calming. And it filled her with a strange longing.

"I just wanted to see what happens with you. You told me about that once, but I had to see for myself. I'm sorry. I wanted to understand how freaked out you get by them."

Her mind calmed along with her body, and she relaxed into him, lulled by his words.

"Malcolm, promise me no more anything with the gags. And I mean the tool as well as the joking. The whole nothing in the mouth thing is critical."

He tilted her head so he could look at her. His eyes were shiny and bright, excited. It dawned on her that he had been fantasizing about this very thing for a long time. He smiled and those sweet lines around his eyes made her melt.

"I promise, no more fooling around. As soon as we walk back into the playroom, it's one hundred percent seriousness."

He removed one hand from her and held up two fingers.

"Scouts honor."

She considered him for another moment and nodded before he guided her back into the room.

"On the table, faceup."

Fiona did as she was told. So far, so good. It felt odd to just be waiting for what came next.

"I thought we would start with something simple, where you are unrestrained."

She had no idea where it had been sitting, but he held up a Violet Wand with a large glass tube at the end. One of her favorite toys, and she knew exactly how painful it could get.

"Um...Malcolm...I mean, Sir...I have an underwire on..."

"Fiona." It was both a direction and a reprimand. She sucked in her lower lip to silence herself and focus.

He turned on the machine, and the familiar buzz of the equipment gave her an unanticipated jolt of excitement. She was like a Pavlovian mouse who knew that good things came out of that sound, but now she was on the receiving end. In spite of that, the anticipation and uncertainty of what he was going to do lit the fire between her legs. The excitement of a wet pussy near an electric wand was exciting no matter which end she was on.

He placed the wand against her chest. The tiniest zap arced through the glass and against her skin and felt just like she'd touched something after walking across shag carpeting on a dry day. Each zap was accompanied by the tiniest intake of breath on her part. Malcolm ran the flickering bulb across her breasts, staying away from the metal on her bra. He lifted it and drew lazy blue pictures over her stomach, each touch a warm-up, a test.

"Methinks a little more." He dialed it up and touched her again on her inner thigh. Her hips jerked upward and off the table. "Ah, yes, that's better."

His little laugh of approval didn't do anything to comfort her. But comfort wasn't his point at the moment. She knew where he wanted to take her, and her body wanted to follow. She tried to focus on her end of the bargain, to be submissive to him. She understood what he was doing by taking one of her favorite tools and using it on her. He had watched her send people into deep subspace with nothing more than the rounded ball filled with argon and a little bit of tinsel draped in strategic locations.

Malcolm moved his head close to hers. He kissed her forehead and laid the glass against the top of her mons and held it there. The electric shock built under the touch and she resisted the urge to cry out.

"Your groans are beautiful, Fiona."

His sonorous voice was lulling, pulling her away from herself and taking her down to where he wanted her. She shifted her hips to push herself up against the wand, seeking an even greater connection in spite of the increasing pain.

"Thank you, Sir." It came out breathy and uncontrolled.

He stepped away to increase the intensity again. This time he pressed the glass against her mons for just a moment before slipping it underneath the top of her panties and catching at the liquid pooling at the opening of her already throbbing cunt. The shock was more intense than anything she'd ever experienced;

her body reacted out of instinct and her hips shot upward as if to knock it away and she screamed.

"Fuck, shit. Stop." But none of these were her safeword. She was stronger than that. She would show him how much she could take. He added more voltage and twisted the glass to dig down to her clit. Her lower body jerked upward, off the table, but he stayed with her, keeping the wand pressed against her, her panties an unusual ally to his efforts. The sharp prickling shocks against her clit threatened to overcome her, but she refused to let him beat her. She focused on trying to please him, to show him what she could handle. She would come soon, if he kept it up.

"May...I...come...Sir?" she managed to squeak out. "Close. So close."

He pulled the wand away.

"No."

She wanted to come. Disappointment flooded through her. She pushed her hips up, hungrily reaching for anything to tip her over the edge, and found only air.

"Please, Sir?"

He sighed and pressed the heel of his palm over her, soothing and stopping her climax at the same time. The warmth and smoothness of his fingers were delicious, and he played with her for a moment, finger-fucking her while she recovered her breath. She could tell he was stroking her down for something else.

"Good girl, Fiona." He held up his fingers to show her the proof of her body's lust and then placed them against her lips.

Fiona's eyes narrowed at him, and she kept her lips compressed into a small tight line. The hell if she would take anything in her mouth—ball gags, fingers, cocks—she didn't use her mouth.

He tilted his head to the side as he watched her response. He outlined her lips with his finger, using little pressure, just languid tracings. She could smell her own scent as he took his time with her.

And that's when it hit her. He had decided on what would be proof of her submission. She would, at some point, take something in her mouth. But, it wouldn't be until she had finally broken for him. Could she do it? She had been close; he'd had her hot and almost ready to break with the Violet Wand shoved against her cunt. If she had dropped into subspace then, would she have been ready?

He reached behind her and brought her up to a sitting position and removed her bra. Her breasts dropped free of the fabric. He let them pool in each hand, his thumbs reaching around to entice the nipples into standing up, erect. He grasped the nipples between thumbs and forefingers and pulled her off the table to guide her into a kneeling position on the floor. He knew she had a bad knee and had put down a yoga mat, folded in half for extra comfort.

"Ah, thank you, Sir," she purred. Malcolm could be such a sweetheart.

"Don't thank me yet."

She shivered with a newfound anticipation and desire. Her whole body ached for completion.

"Head straight, eyes on the wall opposite."

She could hear him opening a drawer and the sound of metal scraping on wood. She turned her head, unable to resist, and he was standing there looking at her with his arms crossed. He shook his head and reached for the blindfold.

"I told you, head straight. Since you seem to be unable to control your desire to look around, I will have to put this on." He dangled the black silk like he was playing with a cat.

She hadn't meant to break his command. It was just natural curiosity to see what he was doing. She sucked in her lower lip and promised herself she would really try. It said something to her that he had the blindfold out before she had arrived. He did know her.

"Yes, Sir. I'm sorry...Sir," she said. She breathed in deeply as he put on the blinder, letting the air out slowly in a long hiss. The darkness engulfed her and put her on edge in a different way. He placed his hands on her shoulders. The warmth sent tendrils of anticipation through her.

"That's better," he said, the exhalation of his breath tickling her earlobe.

And then he was rustling around in the drawers again. The loss of her vision keyed her up a bit, but it also helped her focus. Every sound seemed amplified and alien.

The musical clinking of small chains came closer to her, and she had an idea of what he was about to do. Was she actually smiling?

"Smart girl, aren't you?" he asked. She felt the warmth of his mouth on her nipple, his tongue swirling around the engorged tip. He breathed on it, and the coolness of the air made her shiver. But the clamp, when he placed it on her nipple, dug in deeply and painfully.

Her chin dropped toward her chest as she sucked in a hissing breath.

He lifted her chin.

"Try to keep your head up." His voice had shifted again. Its command and sureness that she was so used to hearing with others was now directed at her. The pain reminded her she had no choice but to simply listen.

"Yes, Sir."

She braced herself as he wet the other nipple in the same way and put on a second clamp. She managed to keep her head up, but this time she let out a loud grunting gasp. Then, as the clamps adjusted around her nipples the pain subsided into a simple tightness. The chain between them dropped against her belly. She had gotten through it without embarrassing herself. The excitement she usually had for watching a sub get through a challenge transposed and shifted into a different level of excitement and a desire to do more for him. To please him with her response.

"Now hold out your hands."

She put her hands out in front of her, wrists together. The hemp rope, she guessed, would be used around her wrists. She waited patiently. The sounds coming from across the room confused her though. Rope wouldn't make any noises like that. That was...

Metal wrist cuffs. The cold hardness of them hit her wrists and tightened around them before she could form the words in her head. He had changed his mind perhaps. Then, she was being pulled to her feet. The movement unsettled her and she almost lost her balance. He caught her by the hips and righted her, holding her close against him. His stiff erection pressed against her.

She whimpered softly, thinking about where she would like him to stuff his cock. She humped against him wantonly, leaving a glistening smear of her desire against the fabric of his pants.

He snorted and stepped back, lifting her arms, and she heard the metal snapping into place around the cuffs, pulling her arms above her head. The metal chain linking her breasts bounced against her belly, sending a searing stream of pain through the clamps.

Cold metal slid along her skin at her hips followed by the decisive swooshing sound of scissors cutting through her panties. Again, cold followed by the sound of steel against steel on the other side and she was completely naked.

"You're pretty hot right now, aren't you?"

"Yes, Sir."

"Did you think you would ever find yourself naked, cuffed to my ceiling like this?"

"No, Sir."

Something tugged at the chains—a finger? She had no way of knowing. The pressure grew and pulled at her nipples. She breathed slowly, taking in the pain. And then he started talking to her. Whispering all those things he said to his regular subs that she had never heard him say before—those private moments of encouragement, a languid mantra of pain and pleasure—telling her how her pain was really her pleasure. And she went with it—she went with him.

The pain in her nipples built with the pleasure between her legs. His finger worked slowly against her clit as he pulled at the chain between her nipples. His singsong voice was hypnotic and utterly convincing. Soon, she was lost in the cadence of his words, looking only to follow his voice out of wherever he had taken her. Between her legs, the desire to come was becoming more than she could bear just as the pain in her nipples was becoming exactly what she had dreamed it could be.

"That's it, Fiona; I don't want you to come until I remove the clamps, then you can let go. The pain will be exquisite." He removed his fingers just as she was about to reach orgasm, and she grunted in frustration, her hips jutting out to find his hand. Even as she pumped against air, he pulled both clamps off of her nipples.

The pain soared through her, and she lost her footing. She grasped at the air with her hands, only to catch herself on the wrist cuffs, as Malcolm caught her around the waist. Then, with the same intensity, the release of the pain swept through her pulsating cunt. She leaned against him, coming against nothing but the desire and pleasure of the pain.

Malcolm's arms were around her, holding her steady as she dropped for the first time ever into subspace. Utter limpness. Fiona knew where she was, but nothing seemed to matter but the ghost energy of her body throbbing in every direction and out of every pore of her skin. If she could draw herself right now, she would look like an angel, with light rays spreading out from every inch of her body. Malcolm removed the blindfold and she met his eyes. They both knew her complete and utter submission had been tendered—they were ready to begin.

MUSE

Lisabet Sarai

Will you sign my copy of your book?"

Her wrist ached from two hours of autographs and she was desperate for caffeine, but she managed a professional smile. "Of course."

The last person in a line that had stretched out the door at the start of the event, he didn't look like her typical reader. His shaggy black hair needed cutting and he could have used a shave. He wore beige zip-up coveralls, a Yankees jacket, and dusty boots. A bit scruffy. Forgettable. His eyes, though, were anything but. They burned in his aquiline face, fierce, passionate, almost crazed. A quiver of unease swept through her. It was a terrible cliché—who would know better than she?—but in the intensity of that stare, she really did feel totally naked.

Smiling more broadly to hide her discomfort, she accepted the paperback he offered. The cover featured a powerfully built man in a leather hood with a scantily clad blonde kneeling at his feet. She flipped to the title page: *Slave to Love by Melissa Appleton*.

"To...?"

"To my Master." He pitched his voice low. No one else could have heard, but that didn't stop hot blood from climbing to her cheeks or sudden moisture from soaking her panties.

"Excuse me, sir, but I don't think..." She peered frantically around the bookstore, at the browsing customers and busy clerk. Nobody had noticed. Some force dragged her back to meet the brazen challenge in his eyes.

"You *should* think, Lissa. Is this what you really want?" He made a dismissive gesture toward the volume on the table. "Knotted silk scarves and soft, sweet kisses? Velvet blindfolds and spanking games? 'Slaves' who surrender for a half-dozen pages, then go about their lives as though nothing has changed?"

"I—my fans—the market..."

"Screw the market." His coarseness made her shudder and yet her nipples snapped into tight, hard peaks as if he'd ordered them to attention. "You want more. I know you do."

He loomed over the table, an undeniable presence despite his no more than average height. She shrank back into her chair, her pulse loud and fast in her ears, her thighs slippery. "I know you, Lissa. I've read every book you've written. I've watched you, on the street, at readings, working at your computer. You don't want timid games. You're afraid to admit it—I understand—but you want marks. Bruises. Blood. You want to be tested, stretched to the breaking point and beyond."

He captured her right wrist in his big, bony hand. The fountain pen fluttered in her fingers like a caged bird. "Write me your fantasies, and I'll make them real. Show me your rawest, darkest dreams—all the filthy details. Then trust me to fulfill them."

Clearly he was mad. Perhaps even dangerous. She should call

Jeremy, the manager, or the security guard who was taking a break now that the crowd had dispersed. Somehow she couldn't move. His grip wasn't tight. She could have pulled her hand away. But his eyes bored into her and his voice stilled her, holding her transfixed like a pinned insect.

"I can't..." she murmured.

"I say you can. If you choose." He leaned closer, until she felt his warm breath on her face. He smelled of tobacco and wood varnish. "It's up to you, Lissa, to take the first step."

"But how...?"

"Begin by writing, *To my Master.*" He relinquished her hand, and she found herself following his instructions. A thrill shot through her as the violet ink she used for signings flowed onto the page. *Master.* So strange. Was this real?

"Good girl. Now, *From his devoted slave.*"

She giggled—she couldn't help herself. It just sounded so silly and cheesy.

"You'll likely find it less amusing as time goes on," he commented, his voice edged with irony.

"Sorry—I just can't take this seriously." She surveyed him with greater care. Amazing that a man of such ordinary appearance could broadcast such an aura of control. Now that she thought of it, his face was somehow familiar. "Is this a joke? Did Laurel put you up to this?" Her best friend, another author, had been known to organize elaborate pranks.

He ignored her question. "Close your eyes."

Without thinking, she obeyed.

"Imagine you're bound tight. Your breasts are purple and sore from the ropes looped around them. A bar is lashed between your ankles, holding you wide open. Your ass is plugged and you're suspended from the ceiling. Your cunt-juice drips onto the floor."

The situation he described sprang to life in her mind, in vivid detail. She was, after all, used to creating scenes out of words. A rush of lust surged through her, leaving her trembling and faint.

"I circle your trussed-up body. I twist your swollen nipples but you can't scream because I've stuffed your mouth with your panties. When I set you swaying, the ropes bite into your flesh. The pain grows."

Her breasts ached from the phantom bonds. Her clit twitched as she pictured the rope rasping between her spread thighs.

"You're beautiful this way, Lissa." His voice was barely audible, close to her ear. "Helpless. Suffering—for me. Wholly and completely mine."

It's not possible to reach orgasm from purely mental stimulation. She knew that; she'd always avoided that trope in her fiction. His intimate whisper triggered *something*, though—if not an orgasm, then something equally sudden and pleasurable that left her shaking in her chair, limp and damp.

She opened her eyes. He hovered beside her, looking over her shoulder, a half smile moderating the intensity of his gaze. "Write it," he ordered. "If you dare. Then bring the book and meet me outside the store. I'll wait for ten minutes."

Without stopping for a reply, he stuffed his hands in his pockets and strode toward the door.

She inhaled deeply, struggling to slow her racing heart. What had *that* been all about? She knew there were plenty of nuts in the city, but this one seemed particularly obsessed with her. Maybe she should ask Jeremy to call her a cab rather than taking the subway.

The book lay open on the table before her. *To my Master.* Her pulse quickened again, despite her best intentions. The plum-colored whorls were stark and elegant. Unfinished. Write it, if you dare.

Of course she'd dreamed of being a slave. That was obvious on a close reading of any of her romances. The passion leaked out, even in the tamest of her kinky scenes. The quality of restraint, of holding back—the ever-present feeling that things might get out of control, go deeper into forbidden territory—this might be responsible for the acute sense of tension often mentioned in her reviews. She'd learned to keep a short leash on her fantasies, after editors made her cut or modify material they judged as too raw for her readers.

My Master. Physically, the guy was nothing like the dominant she'd imagined. Still, he knew how to get under her skin. Mentally replaying their brief interaction made her wetter than ever. Could he truly be what he claimed to be? Could she really trust him enough to surrender?

You can. If you choose.

She glanced at her watch then peered through the plate-glass windows at the front of the store. Darkness had fallen; she couldn't tell whether he was out there on the sidewalk or not.

Words the color of wine. Of bruises. A terrible risk. An opportunity that might never come again.

No time to waste. She seized her pen and scribbled a second line: *From his slave* then signed it *Lissa,* though most people called her Mel. She couldn't bring herself to write *devoted* when he was essentially a stranger. Hopefully he'd be satisfied.

She slipped the volume into her shoulder bag, grabbed her coat and headed for the door. "I'm off, Jeremy," she called to the gangly middle-aged man behind the counter. "Thanks so much for hosting me!"

"Thank *you*, Mel. It was a great crowd—probably a new record! Good thing we stocked up. I think we sold every copy of *Slave to Love* on the shelves and quite a few from your backlist, too."

"Fabulous. Anyway, I'll see you soon..."

"When's your next release? Want to schedule another signing now?"

"April, and no, sorry, but I've got to run. I'll call you. 'Night!"

She hurried out before the voluble manager could delay her further.

Bustling commuters crowded the sidewalk. She twirled on her heels, looking in all directions, but there was no sign of the man in the coveralls. A brisk October wind snarled her hair and pricked up tears in her eyes. She fought the weight of disappointment that settled in her chest as she set out for the subway. She was lucky he was gone. What had she been thinking?

A hand on her arm. A voice in her ear. "Looking for me?"

"Ah—yes—well..." In his presence, her usual verbal ability withered.

"Give me my book."

She fished it out of her bag and handed it to him. In the halo of a streetlight, he checked the inscription. Her face grew hot despite the autumn chill.

"Thank you, Lissa. I'll treasure this." He threaded his arm into hers. "Come with me, then, and we'll begin."

He led her down into the same station she usually used, paid her fare and shepherded her onto her normal train. "I can't take you home with me," she protested. "I have a housemate."

"Yes—I suppose Maria would be quite shocked by what I plan to do with you."

"You—you know Maria?"

"I told you, I know everything about you. Except of course the dark parts you don't share with anyone. But that's about to change."

The car was packed. He clung to a strap behind her and

looped his arm around her waist, with his lean body pressed against her back. Her coat was too bulky to detect whether he was erect, but the mere idea sent her mind spinning in wild directions. She saw herself naked, cuffed to the bar overhead. He fucked her in the ass while the other passengers watched and jeered. After he filled her with spunk, he invited the rest of the train to use her. Businessmen in suits and homeboys with gold chains and droopy jeans, toothless codgers and fresh-faced college guys, everyone wanted a piece of her. They forced her to her hands and knees on the filthy floor and stuffed their cocks into every available orifice. Her Master smiled at the sight of his obedient slave, stretched, gaping, and drenched with cum...

"Here we are."

"What? This is my stop!"

"Mine as well." He continued to guide her, up the stairs, around the corner, onto her own quiet street, lined with vintage brownstones. They came to a stop in front of number 252—her own building.

She pulled away and whirled to face him. "What the hell is going on here? What kind of game are you playing?"

"I told you, Lissa. I don't play games." Rather than climbing the stone steps, he descended the half flight that led to the basement apartment and unlocked the door. He glanced over his shoulder. "Are you coming?"

All at once she knew why he'd seemed familiar. "You—you're the janitor—the maintenance guy—Mike—Mickey..."

"Mitch. Glad to know that I'm not totally invisible."

Shame washed over her. He'd come to her apartment at least once, to fix a problem with a window that wouldn't stay open. She'd barely given him a glance. She'd been working, lost in a scene from one of her books.

"However, from now on, you'll call me 'Master' or 'Sir.'
Understood?"

Irrational relief lightened her heart. He wasn't a total stranger.
Furthermore, his knowledge about her living situation, occupa-
tion and habits didn't derive from some sort of insane stalking.

"Um—yes. I mean, yes, Sir."

She'd written it a hundred times in her sanitized kinky
romances. Saying it out loud was a totally different experience.

Heat sizzled through her. Her nipples plumped. A hungry
gap yawned between her thighs. At the same time, acute embarrassment forced her eyes to the floor.

"Look at me, Lissa."

Difficult as it was, she obeyed.

"Once you cross this threshold, you're mine. My slave to
command, just as you wrote in the inscription."

Terror spiked in her chest. Lust smothered it. "I know, Sir."

"And this is what you want?"

She swallowed hard, nodded.

"Out loud."

"Yes, Sir. This is what I want."

The triumph she read on his face filled her with pride.

"I knew it."

Having stripped her of her clothes, he settled her at a table,
with one ankle cuffed and chained to her chair leg. Within ten
minutes, the chair seat was slick with her pussy juice. He puttered
around the neat, one-room apartment, laying out articles on the
narrow bed: a wooden paddle, a coil of bright red rope, some
silvery metal devices that she assumed must be nipple clamps,
several dildos of various sizes and shapes, an enema bag, a short
whip with dozens of leather strands, each knotted at the end.

With each new item, she grew more aroused and more

agitated. "Are you—are you going to use those on me, Sir?" she blurted out at last.

Her Master grinned. "That's up to you." He handed her a yellow legal pad and a ballpoint pen. "Write out one your darkest fantasies for me. If I think you're being honest, perhaps we'll act it out. I just brought out a few toys to—um—inspire you."

"I—I can't..."

Fisting her hair, he forced her to look into his terrible eyes. "Of course you can. You do it for a living." He indicated a sturdy bookshelf that covered most of one wall. The middle two tiers were crammed with titles by Melissa Appleton. "Only now you don't have to hold back."

Settling into an armchair near the books, he selected a volume (not one of hers), opened it in the middle and proceeded to ignore her.

Frustration roared through her. He wasn't going to touch her? What kind of a Master was he?

She sulked for ten or fifteen minutes, uncomfortably aware that this was not appropriate behavior for a devoted slave. Eventually, she picked up the pen and began to write.

"Sir?"

The room had been silent for so long, her own voice startled her. He looked up from his book.

"Done? Let me see." Seating himself out of reach once again, he perused the three-and-a-half pages she'd composed.

Feeling anxiety mingled with lust, she watched his reactions. He arched an eyebrow—pursed his lips—shook his head. Did he like it? Was it raw enough to earn her the reward she craved?

Finally he set the pad down. His lips curved into a grin. "You certainly are a nasty girl, Lissa. Just as I suspected."

Unzipping his coveralls, he draped them over the chair back. He was naked underneath, sporting a sizable erection that made it quite clear what he thought of her work. Elation sang through her.

"On your knees, slave."

Still shackled to the chair, she was awkward as she slipped to the floor.

"Hands clasped behind you. Back arched." She presented her breasts, wondering what he thought of their modest size. They hadn't really talked about bodies at all. At least her nipples were impressive, pert, fat nubs the size and shape of hazelnuts. He brushed the tips with his palm, sending tendrils of pleasure spiraling down to her clenching pussy.

"Don't move, now. And be quiet."

She'd read about nipple clamps, of course, including personal accounts on BDSM blogs. Her research did not prepare her for the burst of agony when he slid the tines of the tweezer clamp around her nipple and then let go. She bit back her scream, her breathing shallow as she tried to adjust to the excruciating pressure. He pushed the ring circling the tines farther up toward her distorted flesh, tightening the hold. Had she really wanted this? And yet she was soaked, too, her clit pulsing with each surge of pain.

"Very good. Now the other..."

Two clamps hurt far more than twice as much. She whimpered, determined to act like the slave he believed her to be, obedient and brave. He traced the outline of her lips with one finger and then slipped it inside her mouth. She sucked hard on the digit, imagining it was his cock.

"Soon. Very soon. You're doing well, Lissa." He removed his finger, and this time she couldn't stifle her moan. "On all fours now."

Gravity pulled at her breasts, heightening the pain. Mitch unfastened the chain securing her to the chair then backed away. "Crawl to me," he ordered. She did, knowing she looked ridiculous, not caring, if this was what he wanted.

He'd thrown a pillow on the carpet. With a hand between her shoulder blades, he pressed her head to the floor. "Stretch your arms back behind you." She'd complied before he'd even finished the order. This was, after all, her fantasy.

She'd imagined rope, but instead he fastened leather cuffs around her wrists and ankles, then clipped the upper and lower limbs together. It didn't matter. She was effectively immobilized, at his mercy—just as she craved.

Next came the butt plug. He made her suck it first, while he fingered her rear hole. Then he forced it into her anus, without any lube other than her saliva. He was following her script to the letter. The lush, shameful sense of fullness almost balanced the tearing pain in her over-stretched flesh—almost.

"Ready for the cat?" he asked.

"Ah—oh—what if I said 'no,' Sir?"

"I'd flog you anyway, slave."

His answer pleased her.

The thongs whirred as he whisked them through the air, then bit into her flesh like a hundred red-hot needles. He lashed her again and again. Searing lines of fire stitched across her skin. She jerked and moaned as the leather strands danced across her flesh, helpless to escape from his pitiless onslaught. She hated every instant. She didn't want him to stop. And even if she had—it would have made no difference.

"You'll have marks for days." He smoothed his calloused hand over her battered ass, waking echoes of his strokes. The whip kissed her again. "Beautiful stripes, and welts from the knots."

She nearly came at the thought.

Finally, when she was drunk on the combination of pain and pleasure, he rolled her onto her back, with her arms still fastened to her legs, and rammed his cock into her drenched cunt. The force of his thrusts ground her punished rear against the carpet and pushed the plug farther into her anus. A climax seized her, welling up from depths she hadn't known existed.

With some last shred of self-consciousness, she realized that slaves don't come without permission, that he'd punish her for this transgression. That just triggered a second orgasm.

Mitch and Lissa strolled down 12th Street in the summer dusk. His arm circled her waist, proprietary and comforting.

"Hey, Lissa, look! Sandman Books already has the book." Sure enough, there in the window of the store where they'd met was a pile of hardback volumes. The elegant cover displayed a shadowy swell of flesh that might or might not be a woman's buttocks, draped with single length of silver chain. *A Slave's Secrets,* read the title. *By Melissa Appleton.*

"Looks fantastic, doesn't it? I read that the fundamentalist organizations plan to picket every bookstore in the city next week to protest the sale of your 'filth.' That should help sales."

She smiled to herself. He had a right to be proud. It was his accomplishment as much as hers. She would never have taken the next step, if he hadn't encouraged her...

"Is it sore, pet?" Her Master's voice interrupted her musings.

Her cotton skirt fluttered around her legs. Underneath, her bare pussy throbbed from her recent labial piercing—far more painful than when she'd done her nipples.

"You know it is. You love the fact, too."

He leaned in and nipped her earlobe.

"Ow!"

"You're right, I do. But aren't you forgetting something, slave?"

"What—oh, sorry—you love the fact, *Sir.*"

"Are you being insolent? Trying to make me punish you?"

"That would never occur to me, Sir."

His grin reassured her that punishment or not, she'd get what she wanted—as long as she was brave enough to ask.

POSTCARDS
FROM PARIS

Giselle Renarde

E mily's heart raced. From the moment Yannik walked in, she couldn't sit still.

"Go ahead," Hunter said with a smirk. "Give the guy a hug."

Emily raced across the restaurant and wrapped her arms around Yannik's neck. "You're here!" She knocked off his top hat when she reached up to kiss his cheek. "Oops, sorry."

"You look lovely," Yannik said, as Emily picked up his hat. "That velvet's a great color."

"Got it at the consignment shop." She handed Yannik his hat and then gave a twirl. "How about *you*? You look very dapper in your tails."

"Why thank you," he said, with a debonair bow.

Emily couldn't get over how good it was to have Yannik back in town. She and Hunter had missed him so much while he was in France. The house wasn't the same with just the two of them.

"Would you lovebirds get over here?" Hunter called from the table. "Come keep me company. I'm getting lonely all by myself."

Emily led Yannik to the table by the window. Before taking his seat, he kissed Hunter firmly on the mouth. Other patrons took notice, and that used to make Emily uncomfortable. Now it made her unabashedly proud.

"How did it go at the airport?" Hunter asked.

"Same old, same old." Yannik set his hat on the extra chair and picked up a menu. "They took me into one of those little rooms to question me about the packer."

"Did they make you take your pants off?" Emily asked.

"No, thank god. The gal who came to interview me was really apologetic that I got targeted. She said they've all been trained in screening transpeople, and some of her colleagues are just assholes."

Emily laughed. "She actually said that?"

Yannik nodded.

"Fuck, it's just a fake cock," Hunter said. "I don't know why they get so worked up."

The waiter cleared his throat. "Are we were ready to order?"

Emily bit her lip and tried not to grin as the boys ordered dinner. She knew how funny the three of them looked—the men divinely overdressed in vintage tuxedos, she wearing a gown from the twenties and a peacock feather in her hair.

"So, what did you bring us?" Emily asked when the waiter was gone. "I've been looking forward to some fancy French souvenirs."

"Yes, yes," Hunter chimed in. "Perhaps some fine lingerie for the lady?"

Smirking, Yannik reached into his breast pocket. "Postcards from Paris!"

"Postcards?" Emily said. "That's it?"

"These ones are special." Yannik spread them across the table. "They're roughly turn-of-the-century."

Emily glanced around the dining room to make sure nobody else could see. The postcards were very naughty: saucy ladies, naked or half-dressed, lesbian spankings and threesomes...

"Would you look at this one!" Hunter pointed to a nude with a particularly full bush. "You don't see that anymore."

"No indeed," Yannik agreed. "They're all like that, to some degree. A nice natural bush on a nude marked the photograph as erotic."

"Really?" Emily picked up the card Hunter had been drawn to. How could anyone be so hairy?

"Well, think about Old Master paintings," Yannik said. "You don't see pubic hair in classical art pieces. Pussies are kind of...*whitewashed*, I guess. The big, full bushes set these postcards apart from high art. A hairy pussy was meant to titillate."

Emily cringed at the thought of having that much hair inside her panties. "I don't know about that. I like a shaved pussy."

"Yes, we've noticed," Yannik said, looking at Hunter as though they were conspiring in some way. "I think we'd both like to see you...au naturel."

The waiter came by to fill their water glasses and Emily blushed like he could see through her clothes. The boys didn't seem ashamed in the least. They didn't even pack up the post-cards.

When the waiter went away, Emily asked, "You're going to take away my razor, aren't you?"

"The moment we get home," Hunter said as Yannik kissed her cheek.

* * *

It was unbearably itchy, growing in. Emily squirmed all day
for the first few weeks. Every time she showered, she plotted
to steal Hunter's razor out of the medicine cabinet. This wasn't
fair. She was uncomfortable all day, and why? Because the boys
decreed it.

But Emily could never bring herself to shave. She knew
how disappointed they'd be if she went against their word.
The punishment would be a moratorium on discipline, and
she couldn't bear it. She couldn't go a day without their loving
straps or spankings.

Ultimately, Emily was glad she held out. After a couple
weeks, her crotch stopped itching so much. A month later, she'd
cultivated a respectable bush. The boys took note. They got out
a ruler and measured the length. They compared her with the
women in the postcards. After a good two months of growing it
out, Emily was really rather pleased with herself.

The boys were pleased, too.

"I've never seen this much hair on a woman," Yannik said,
in that dark voice that made Emily shiver.

Hunter helped him tie her wrists to her legs, spread-eagled
on the couch. Her thighs trembled. She thought she couldn't
hold the pose, at first. And then, as other things distracted her,
the ache subsided.

"It's dark," Hunter said. "I'm surprised. I thought it would
be closer to your hair color, but it's almost black, isn't it?"

"Almost," Emily said, wincing. They always did this—
ignored her pain, pretended she was perfectly at ease in whatever position they picked. Didn't matter that her muscles were
twitching, stretching, crying out in pain. That's what they
wanted.

"Look how wet she is," Yannik said, patting her pussy.

"How can you tell?" Hunter asked. "I can't see a thing beyond that fucking hair."

All Emily could think was, *Don't act so disgusted by my body. You made me do this!* But she bit her lip. She didn't speak.

"There's so much of it." Yannik traced his fingers through her bush, making it stick up like a Mohawk so she looked ridiculous.

They played with her pussy like it was a toy. She wanted to feel embarrassed about all that goddamn hair, but she also loved the attention. Two men, four eyes, ten fingers focused on her hairy little cunt. But the boys' humiliation plot was sagging just a touch, because she *liked* it.

"You're right," Hunter said, shoving one finger up her snatch. "Wow, she *is* wet."

Of course I'm wet! You put on my black stay-up stockings, you split me open, tie my wrists to my legs and start teasing me? How could I not be wet?

"Take your finger out," Yannik said to Hunter. "I want to do something."

The moment Hunter withdrew his finger from Emily's cunt, Yannik spanked it. He smacked her pussy with three fingers, hard enough for a wet echo to ring through the living room. There was nothing she could do to resist. She couldn't move. Her muscles ached, but she remained in the wide-open position they'd chosen for her.

"I love that sound," Hunter said. "Spank her pussy again."

Yannik smacked her without delay, just barely catching her flesh. Her hair acted as a buffer, which was such a tease.

"Again," Hunter encouraged. "Harder."

The next blow warmed her cunt enough that she wondered if her skin was getting red down there. Impossible to see.

"Open her pussy for me," Yannik said. "I want to see the pink."

Hunter growled as he grabbed Emily's lips and parted them roughly. No, that wasn't good enough—not for Hunter. He clutched her pussy hair and pulled, sending shocks through her body. If she arched forward, she could just make out the deep pink of her wet flesh. Hunter was mostly blocking her view, and he was also pulling on her bush so hard her vision started to blur.

"Watch your fingers," Yannik said to Hunter before spanking Emily's clit.

The first blow was off. It fell to the side. He tried again, and clipped her clit sharply this time. An electric pulse shot through her body. She arched forward, but there was nowhere to go without folding herself into a pretzel.

"That hurt, did it?" Hunter asked.

Emily bit her lip, nodding.

"Yannik." The boys made eye contact, and Hunter commanded, "Do it again."

Another sharp slap met her bare pussy, and she threw herself back against the couch. Her thighs screamed for a second, then got warm. Her pussy was glowing when he hit it again, catching her clit off guard. Her ass tightened up as a burst of lightning surged through her arms. Her heart raced. All of her body was connected to her clit—spank it and everything reacted.

Yannik offered a steady stream of spankings. "I wonder how long I can do this before she starts to cry."

Ahh, the power of suggestion...

Either Yannik's blows were falling harder, or Emily's flesh had been as tenderized as she could handle. Tears welled in her eyes. She bit her lip hard to keep quiet.

"Use something else besides your hand," Hunter said, egging

Yannik on. They always played this way—boys against girl, plotting every way to torture her. "Get the crop. That'll work perfect."

"Ooh, yeah." Yannik jumped up and raced to the spare room, where all their sexual paraphernalia was kept.

Hunter had been staring at her pussy all this time, but he looked into her eyes now. Something about the angular line of his jaw made her heart beat a little faster, especially when he smiled in that conniving way of his. Emily blinked, and her tears fell in searing streaks down her cheeks.

"I don't think we're ever going to let you shave again," Hunter said, pressing two fingers inside her swollen cunt. Two, then three. Emily whimpered when he rubbed that spot inside—the G-spot so many people claimed didn't exist. Well, something was in there, and Hunter had no problem finding it. She whimpered as he stroked her.

"Uh-oh," Yannik said, standing behind Hunter with his unassuming black crop. "Looks like someone's enjoying herself a little too much."

Hunter grinned. "Wouldn't want that. Emily's already spoiled, living with two hot guys."

"Guys who buy her vintage gowns and take her to fancy dinners," Yannik replied. "Emily's the most spoiled little girl I've ever met."

"Same here," Hunter said, as he fucked her with his fingers. "We give her everything she needs and all she does is take, take, take."

"Greedy, greedy girl." Yannik whisked Hunter's fingers out of the way and loomed between her legs. "Greedy girl deserves a smack."

She'd been smacked a good many times already, by Yannik's own hand, but she wouldn't remind him. Emily knew how to behave. She could keep her mouth shut with the best of them.

Yannik slid the small tongue of his crop between her spread legs. Emily could feel her slick wetness coating the black leather as he drew it up to her clit, then back down again. Her pussy was sopping, dripping juice along her asscrack. She missed being able to see what was going on down there, that gorgeous leather sliding against her bare flesh, but the longer she grew out her bush, the more affection she felt for it—like a crop she'd cultivated herself, and could take pride in. There sure was a lot of hair.

"I hope you're ready for this," Yannik said, and brought the crop down hard.

Emily cringed even before the leather tongue touched her. The desperate cry it made as it whipped through the air was more than enough to send the fear of god through her body. She tried to close her legs, but her bindings made it too difficult. All she could manage was to roll so the crop caught her hairy pussy rather than her glistening, cherry-red clit.

"Oh, Em, that was not smart." Yannik stood back for a moment. "If you can't be trusted to keep still, you know what's in store."

She stared at him, no response. Her heart clambered into her throat. It was all she could hear as Hunter climbed onto the couch. Facing away from her, he straddled her body, and held her legs open by the ankles. Once he'd found a good position, he set his weight on her so she couldn't struggle. All she could see now was the back of his T-shirt. All she could feel was his grip around her ankles. His fingers were still wet with her juice.

"Hold her good and still." Yannik traced that little leather tongue up and down Emily's splayed pussy. It was such a tease, not being able to see. The suspense was torture enough.

And then Yannik slapped her clit with the crop, and she screamed bloody murder because, god, it hurt. It hurt like hell.

Her tender pussy blazed, sending explosions right through her nervous system. The pain was so severe she thought about using her safeword. She thought about it, but...Christ, she wanted more. She did.

Hunter gripped her ankles a little harder as Yannik whipped her pussy—twice, this time, in rapid succession. The first one didn't even register until the second strike hit. Then, her hips bucked without her consent, and Hunter sat heavier on her belly, molding her body around his, and driving her back into the soft couch cushions, for which she was thankful.

She didn't realize she was mumbling until Yannik hushed her. What had she been saying? *It hurts. It hurts. I can't stand it. It hurts so much...*

Yannik struck her again, and she wished to god she could see her clit. It felt utterly distended, as big as a cherry. Did it look that way, or were her nerve endings blowing things out of proportion?

Between strikes, her pussy seemed to absorb all the cool air in the room. Her clit was blazing. It hurt. Why did she want more of this? She must be crazy.

"Do it again," Hunter encouraged. "I love the way she shakes when you hit her clit. Her whole body trembles."

"Does it?" Yannik brought the crop down on her pussy. This time, instead of just smacking her clit and moving the leather tongue away, he left it there, pressing squarely against her clit.

"It burns!" she screamed. Emily always tried to keep quiet while the boys were working her over, but she couldn't manage that now. Her body was blazing, like her pussy had caught fire. "Fuck, it hurts! It burns!"

"Really?" Yannik asked, slapping her again, with that same callous trick of leaving the crop flush to her clit. "It burns?"

"Yes!" Emily was crying, sobbing. They obviously couldn't

see her face, but couldn't they hear it in her voice? "Guys, it's killing me. It hurts so much!"

"This does?" *Smack.* "This hurts?" *Smack.* "A lot?" *Smack.*

"I can't take it anymore!" Tears coursed down her cheeks as Hunter pressed his back against her face. His spine dug into her cheek, but that was the least of her concerns. "It hurts so fucking much!"

"It hurts, huh?" Yannik smacked her dispassionately, like he was doling out a predetermined punishment. Every strike was measured, metronomic. He played her body like an instrument. Every blow made her sing.

"It hurts," she sobbed into Hunter's back. His shirt absorbed the mess as her nose ran and her tears flowed. She was even drooling on him, because she couldn't manage to close her mouth between sobs. Her words weren't words anymore, just a steady stream of, "Ahhh."

"Think she's had enough?" Yannik asked Hunter. He traced the leather tongue around the perimeter of her pussy, like he was mowing her pubic hair from the outside in. "Maybe she's forgotten her safeword."

"Has Emily forgotten her safeword password?" Hunter asked, loosening his grip on her ankles.

"No." Emily wiped her face across Hunter's back. "I didn't forget."

"Well," Yannik said solemnly. "Sometimes daddies know best."

Hunter bowed to her pussy and spit. That soft drizzle landed like a balm against her clit, soothing her blazing flesh. Part of her wanted more from the crop. It hurt like fuck, but crying was cathartic. She loved sobbing wildly while her men destroyed her. But she trusted them above all else. If they said she'd had enough, she'd had enough.

Yannik untied her wrists, but warned, "I wouldn't close your legs, if I were you."

When Hunter rose from on top of her, Emily got her first glimpse at her hot, red pussy. It looked even more engorged than it felt. She must be seeing things wrong. How could her little pussy possibly look so distended? So fat and red and ripe?

"Sit still and relax," Hunter said. He left the room while Yannik turned on the radio, and reappeared with a damp cloth. When he set it against her blazing cunt, she let out a sigh because nothing had ever felt so good.

Emily sat with her legs wide open, and Yannik settled on the floor between them, kissing her thighs while Hunter sang along with the radio.

"Hey, is there something on my back?" he asked Emily, sitting beside her on the couch. "My shirt feels all wet."

"I don't know, man." She bit her lip to keep from snickering. "Maybe you were sweating a lot."

Yannik shook his head. He knew her too well. "How's your pussy feeling?"

"Still hurts," she said as Hunter adjusted the cloth against her mound. "You know what's weird? I'm really starting to like all this hair."

"I had a feeling you would." Yannik glanced at the wall above the couch, where he'd hung his postcards from Paris. "Growing a full bush is a lost art, but the impact is just as erotic in person as it was in those photographs, if you ask me."

"Me too," Hunter replied, looking up at the postcards.

Emily couldn't see the cards from where she was sitting. Instead, she gazed between her legs, into the dark bush she'd cultivated out of nothing. With a smile, she said, "Me three."

FLIGHT

Cela Winter

Heat from the waning day radiated from the asphalt, raising with it tired smells of car exhaust, dust and garbage. Her skin felt sticky under the cotton dress. Overhead, heat lightning sliced across the amassing gray clouds that hastened the nightfall.

Jane wondered if he had found the note yet. A small shiver of anticipation stroked her spine, in spite of the sultry air.

The cramped motel room didn't offer much for entertainment. Apparently, even the Gideons had no use for such a place, and the aimless waiting was making her anxious, so she'd wandered out to the street. She bought an ice-cream bar thinking to cool off a bit, but threw it away after a couple of bites. Her stomach was just too tense.

Pawnshops, boarded-up windows, tired-looking cafés: the neighborhood was even less inviting at dusk than by day, but then the very seediness was part of the point, a form of camouflage. Streetlamps—those that still functioned—began coming on as the light faded. The gaps between seemed all the darker by contrast and she hurried from each pool of light to the next, like a small, timid animal, like a mouse.

Mouse. That was *his* name for her, a comment on her bashful ways, her petite frame and the quiet brown of her hair. A pet name of sorts, among other names.

His voice, low and intense: "You like that, don't you? Don't you, dirty girl? Squeak for me, little Mouse."

They were such a contrast as a couple. His height and physical power, his vitality, were what initially caught her eye, startling her with the pull of attraction from a man she wouldn't have considered her type. Jane's shoulders twitched, alive with the memory of his hand resting on the nape of her neck. Her previous life hadn't prepared her for meeting someone like Alan.

Exclamations and gasps. The shock of flesh striking flesh, the sharp charge of adrenaline starting from the point of contact then surging through her.

The thought halted her, abrupt as a glass wall in her path. As possessed by the need to return to the room as she had been to leave it earlier, she wheeled and hurried back, her footsteps sounding loud in her ears.

Up ahead, the fitful neon of the motel sign—the LUCKY DICE INN—was a cliché from a grind house movie. Part of the *D* was burned out, making it LUCKY LICE. It was the sort of dive she ordinarily would pass by without a glance or a thought. Certainly it was the last place anyone would expect to find her—Plain Jane, Jane the mouse, respectable and predictable, faculty wife, soccer mom, secret reader of racy romances. It made an unlikely haven, but the rates were low; in her impulsive flight from the house, she'd come away without much cash.

A slap to the ass, the face, the cunt. The sound of fabric tearing, a cry quickly stifled.

A gust of wind chased her up the stairs, belling out her skirt and swirling around her bare legs. Had the overhead light been out when she left? She couldn't remember. Glad to be off the street, she slid the old-fashioned key into the lock and was partway across the threshold before realizing that the door swung too easily.

It was already open.

There was a frozen moment, half a breath, as her body tried to decide what to do, then a hand clamped on her wrist and pulled her in. The snick of the latch shut away the outside world. There was only him...and her...and the dark.

The shock went to her legs and she would have fallen if not for the fingers woven though her hair, cradling the back of her head. Sweat popped out all over her. She thought she could smell herself, acrid with the tensions of the day and the odor of the street. He leaned in close, looming, his face a finger's width from hers. With eyes growing accustomed to the lack of light she saw his lips move, but the thunder—or was it her own heart's thudding?—drowned out the words, not that she really needed to hear them.

"Alan, I—" She heard it before she felt it, the crack of his palm impacting her cheek, then the blossom of pain as her head jolted back, eyes burning with tears.

"Speak when I tell you, Mouse." Her ears were working again. His voice was cold, taut with restraint, the dispassionate tone affecting her more than if he'd raged or threatened. The pieces of her life separated, rearranged themselves and reformed...and she became fully the *other* Jane, the one who'd been waiting all day.

There was pressure on the top of her head, compressing her neck, forcing her knees to bend till they landed on the gritty carpet. Haltered by his grip in her hair, her face was pressed into the fly of his jeans. Semi-hard already, his denim-covered erection grew as he rubbed it against her, dragging her lips back and forth across her teeth.

"You know what to do, dirty girl."

With unsteady fingers, she worked open the button and parted the zip fly. She closed her eyes, inhaling the *Alan* smell—clean cotton, his soap, the muskiness of his balls—and letting it eddy in her brain. Carefully, she tugged down his jeans and shorts, easing the elastic over his rigid cock, allowing it to spring free.

He flexed and the mushroom head butted against her mouth. "Show how much you love your husband, Jane." She paused for a moment, tantalizing herself with the delay and trying to swallow with a throat suddenly dry with desire.

The hesitation earned another slap to the face. "And act like you like it."

Obediently, she opened and took a tentative lick, then another. The parched tissues of her mouth flooded with saliva at the taste of the salty drop on his tip. Alan hissed as she circled his retracted foreskin, then she sealed her lips around him. Breathing shallowly through her nose, she relaxed her throat and took him in deeply a fraction at a time, moving her head in rhythm with his hips.

An image came to her mind of a slight woman kneeling before a well-built man, under his control, doing his bidding, humbly making a gift of her submission.

A moan of pure want sounded from way down in her chest; she couldn't help it. Her arms circled his upper thighs, clinging to him; her fingers dug into his buttocks, nails gripping the firm flesh as she lavished him with her tongue before drawing him back in with a steady suck.

"Stop."

She froze.

"You don't get out of this that easily. I won't be done with you for a while yet." He disengaged. "On the bed. Now. All fours. Legs spread."

She didn't need to be encouraged a second time. She scuttled to obey...and waited.

The mattress was cheap and old, the uncertain support making it difficult to stay still, but he hadn't told her she could move. Her ears strained, trying to decipher the soft sounds behind her. She felt the bed dip under his weight, but still he did nothing. Her muscles began to tremble with tension, her insides aching.

Then her face was mashed into the musty, sex-smelling bedspread. Her skirt was flipped up; there was the pull of nylon and elastic, panties stretching and biting into the crease of her thigh then breaking, leaving her bared.

A sharp smack to one side of her ass surprised a yelp from her. "Quiet! That's for running." A blow to the other side, and that time she was able to muffle her response. "That's for making me come after you." Another, then another, alternating right and left; she lost count as her flesh heated up and her muscles stopped resisting, the boundaries of her mind and body blurring into pure sensation.

Then he was shoving into her with a swift, single motion, giving her no time to prepare, no opportunity to adjust to the stretch of his girth inside her.

"No—no. Not ready. I—" But it was only a token protest, a convention of the game. Her body plainly gave the lie to her words with the wild, liquid warmth that welled between her legs mixing with the remains of her saliva on his cock.

The fucking was steady, patient, relentless. Heat coiled inside her, demanding momentum, and Jane ground her teeth, resisting the primal urge to move, to match his thrusts.

An arm clamped across her stomach, forcing out her breath. Alan levered himself upright on his knees, pulling her with him, pinned to his chest, his cock slipping out of her with a meaty sound. Instinctively, she caught at it, not wanting to lose the contact, rubbing it between her pussy lips as she arched and swayed.

His forearm kept her pinioned; the other hand groped against the front of her dress and jerked open the buttons. He fumbled at her bra, yanking the cup down to expose her breast. His open palm brushed the erect nipple, a whisper of a touch that only her heightened senses allowed her to feel, then she cried out from the vicious pinch of his fingers, twisting, nails biting into her soft flesh.

"My dirty girl likes it rough, doesn't she?"

She could only nod, beyond words, feeling small against his strength, letting that welcome vulnerability carry her along in their potent battle of love and violence. Moisture trickled from her opening, and her movements on his cock sped up. She pushed the ball of her hand to her clit, grinding against herself, angling her hips for better friction.

His breath was hot at the curve where shoulder met neck; she felt the lingering softness of a kiss, then the sharp pressure of his teeth, almost meeting through the skin. The thrill of pain and surrender shot through her as if sparks were flying from her nipples, zinging straight to her cunt.

Jane was soaring, spiraling over and over from a great height. Only Alan's supporting arm, like an iron bar across her middle, kept her from collapsing onto the bed.

Her chest was still heaving, her insides quivering when he released her and flipped her over to her back. Grasping an ankle in either hand, he tipped her backward, heels almost to her ears, exposing her completely.

"Look at me. I want to see your expression when I fill you up." She blinked open hazy eyes.

Alan's steely control of earlier was gone and he pistoned into her, the cords of his neck straining, sweat dripping from his face to land on her bared chest. The bed squeaked and thumped, the underwire of the skewed brassiere dug into her ribs, her hip joints protested at the pounding they were taking as he plunged in and out.

She loved it.

She loved being his vessel for pleasure, loved that Alan could be the man he really was with her, that she was woman enough to take it—and meet it, on her own terms.

The blank, dry years before they met, when the shocking things in her mind tormented her, when her stumbling attempts to express her yearnings to boyfriends came to nothing, or else drove them away.

Her true life began when she met Alan.

Tears of mingled pain, joy, relief flowed from the corners of her eyes, running down her temples into her hair. She tried to match his movements, but couldn't get enough traction, her hands scrabbling at the bedding. Above her, his face changed, flushed, eyes bulging, a mask of greedy lust, the thrusts becoming still wilder and more erratic as the climax took him. His lips moved, forming one word over and over.

"Mine. Mine. Mine."

His. His. His.

Another ripple of response took her over from the inside, twisting tight, tighter, then springing free. Jane followed it, her body bucking up off the mattress.

"Fuck. Dirty. Fuck. Dirty. Dirty. Dirty girl." The words sobbed from her, one for each contraction deep within.

At last they were still, huffing and gasping till their breathing returned to normal. Alan rolled off her and she gave an inadvertent moan of relief; he *was* heavy. With soft kisses to her face and throat, he gently unbent her stiffened legs, massaging the joints, whispering praises for her strength and courage. Her consciousness began to seep back to reality, regrounding itself after her flight from the house and the mind-shift necessary to suspend disbelief and play the game.

Her previous life hadn't prepared her for meeting someone like him. Alan didn't think she was unbalanced or perverted. He listened, really listened, and helped her find her way.

He paused to suckle softly at her abused nipple. For a moment it was soothing, just for a moment, then a flick of his tongue sent a spear of sensation through her body. She sighed with the pleasure, too spent to pursue the feeling, but promising herself more after a rest.

The bed shifted as he got up. There was a snap and the feeble, low-watt bulb in the bathroom flickered on.

"Good god, Jane, this place is a dump! You sure picked a great spot to go to ground."

She laughed, her throat raspy from panting. "Yes, it is fairly disgusting isn't it? But don't you think that kind of adds to the—" A curse from the bathroom interrupted her.

"There're bugs in here!"

"We'll be lucky if there aren't bugs in the bed." A mumble and the sound of urine hitting the toilet were the answer.

Her ass tingled and she shifted, trying to find a comfortable position, then let herself drift for the moment, sinking her awareness into the heavy rubberiness of her limbs. From long habit, she took a mental inventory. Everything ached. Her face felt tight and hot from the slaps, crusty with tears, chafed from contact with the bedspread; then there was her still-smarting nipple and the bite on her shoulder. She could see it in her mind, blossoming angry red with violet teeth marks like the most primal tattoo. His mark.

She felt him return and sit beside her. "Where are the kids?" she murmured.

"Dropped 'em off at my mom's. I told her we were going on a couple's retreat with the church." Jane couldn't help chortling at that—she felt anything but holy at the moment.

"Mmm," she hummed as he soothed the skin of her face with a warm, damp cloth, wiping away the mess of tears and snot and saliva, before moving down to tenderly clean between her legs. She hissed and twitched at the contact, more than a little raw. She realized she was smiling.

"Y'know, Jane, even this washcloth is threadbare."

"Okay, okay. So next time I'll go to the Hilton. You might find it a little harder to break into a room there, though. That was very well done, by the way. How'd you manage it?"

"Oh, I had a little chat with the manager plus some persuasion from my old friend Mr. Jackson."

"Mr. who? Oh, a *twenty*? That's not much of a bribe."

"It isn't much of a place, babe." Footsteps and raucous laughter sounded from outside the flimsy door and passed on. "Does this establishment even do any all-night business?"

"Well, now—" Indignation prompted Jane to defend herself, but he shushed her to silence. In a single lithe move, he straddled her on hands and knees with her wrists flattened against the bed under his palms.

"Actually, Mouse, your choice, such as it is, has certain advantages." He drew a line between her breasts and up her throat with the tip of his nose, ending with his lips next to her ear. In a whisper, he continued, "No one is likely to notice a few screams."

SAVORING
LITTLE ONE

Graydancer

There are specific delights about kinky play that, like the notes of a fine wine, you don't notice until you've become a connoisseur. You have to become attenuated through prolonged exposure to get past the puerile, *Heh, ASS!* stage.

As I sat there regarding the petite and demure delight standing by her front door, I appreciated the finer notes of her nervous weight shifting from foot to foot, anxious, smiling, aroused and excited and caught between *"Oh my god, what have I invited in?"* and *"Oh my god, it's going to happen!"* Probably she half-expected to be thrown over my knee as if we were in some bodice-ripper novel, skirt flipped up and panties down as the walloping commenced.

That approach has merit, to be sure, and while I've never embraced the full Daddy/girl dynamic there is a certain *frisson* of sexiness to domestic discipline. Hell, it doesn't even have to be domestic—John Wayne as McLintock teaching Maureen O'Hara the error of her ways in the Wild West, that's enough masturbatory fodder for years.

I know this for a fact.

However, that was not what I had in mind for her this evening. Our times together were too infrequent, her alabaster skin too pure and precious a thing to hurry the experience. No, this needed to be savored, and that meant we would move slowly.

I saw her eyes flit around the room, not so much looking for escape—she'd invited me here, after all. Now her self-imposed captivity had transformed into an erotic, nervous excitement. She was still at the door where she'd fastened the bolts and turned the lights out. I'd given her that command as I'd entered, and it had the effect I'd intended. The curtains were open and the moon, street and automobile lights flickered across the silver-lit room.

More importantly, she had complied. A good start. "Turn around," I commanded, not so much because I expected obedience but more to gauge her reaction.

Two things happened—there was an involuntary twist to her body, as if her first inclination had been to obey. This was followed by a flush of blood to her cheeks, a slight pursing of her lips in defiance as she caught herself. I could almost hear her inner monologue saying that she wasn't going to be *that* easy, she was going to make sure I had to work for it.

I gave a theatrical sigh at her defiance, but inwardly I was delighted. I love having to work for it; it is truly a labor of lust.

Besides, I knew that she *was* going to be that easy.

I rose from the chair with a smooth, predatory grace, very different from the travel-weary slump with which I'd sat down. Her eyes widened and she gave a slight start, as if to run. I smiled. Adrenaline is a wonderful thing, and at that moment it was making her wonder what had happened to the tired, middle-aged white guy she thought had walked into her apartment.

Three quick steps and I was close, closer than was socially acceptable, but still not touching. We weren't quite face-to-face. I didn't want her to have the comfort of confrontation. I loomed, towering over her, the center of my chest less than an inch from the tip her nose, slightly to the left. I had gambled that she wouldn't move, wouldn't look up, and it was a good bet. In the world of "fight, flight, freeze or fuck," we were solidly in the realm of the last two.

I smelled her hair, intoxicating so close to my face, but I didn't let any of my desire into my voice as I tilted my head down.

In a low, controlled tone, I began. "I'm going to tell you to do a lot of things tonight, Little One. You get to choose whether you would like to simply do them..." I reached up to lay my hand on her shoulder, my thumb curling under the swell of her clavicle. "Or do them painfully." My thumb dug in as I pushed, pivoting her around.

I stepped in, closing the gap between us as her body turned, letting my body maintain her balance as my arm folded across her chest, maintaining the pressure against her clavicle.

She gasped, both at the pain and the sudden sensation of my warmth pressing against the entire back of her body. She pressed back into me, out of involuntary desire and the need to escape the point of pain at her shoulder. I gave no respite, hugging her closer, treating myself to a nuzzle in the gossamer rustle of hair. Gradually I reduced the pressure from my thumb, letting her breath calm, though I kept her close with my arm and my voice was millimeters from her ear.

"Rest assured, though, everything I command will be done. To my complete"—I suddenly released my grip and stepped back, leaving her to totter for a moment—"satisfaction."

I stood there a moment, waiting, daring her to turn her head to look at me. In our previous play I'd never slapped her face, not yet, but it was explicitly allowed in the negotiations that had led to this evening. She knew that. I would not hesitate if she gave me reason. I suspected she knew that too.

I suspected the thought made her wet.

There were a lot of things that had been negotiated for this evening, things that perhaps she was having second thoughts about. But for now, we were savoring this precious tango of wills. She could always safeword out, but we were nowhere near that. I smiled as I watched her square her shoulders and straighten her spine, standing a bit taller.

I gave her a silent *Atta girl!* accolade, but out loud I simply said "Are we clear?"

There was a long, intensifying silence before she replied with her petite alto, "Yes, Sir."

"Good." Seizing the momentum, I upped the ante. "Lift your skirt for me."

This time she didn't hesitate, nor did I expect her to. Not because I'd won, no; simply because she's a smart woman who knows how to pick her battles. This was one she could let go and bide her time until a better opportunity presented for her to show how in-control she was.

I looked forward to that moment. It would be yet another opportunity for us both to enjoy the struggle and her inevitable submission. It wasn't that I was unstoppable. It was that everything we did was predicated on the same goal: giving her the freedom to lose control, to relax into someone else's will. My will.

Her defiance now was already undermined by the fifth column of her desire to give her body and spirit to me. The goal was never in doubt. There was simply the journey to enjoy.

I watched the hem of her skirt rise as she bunched it, fistful by fistful, at her waist. Her calves flexed atop the precarious heels, elegantly simple black stilettos. The delicate curves of muscle were split by the seam of each smooth stocking and in the ambient light of the Amsterdam streets they shone argent like brushed aluminum.

The fabric went higher, revealing the delicate backs of her knees. I licked my lips with the hunger to kiss each hollow, to feel her tremble beneath me. I flexed my hands, wanting to grasp her, take her now, but I made no move.

Slow. Savor.

Her thighs came into view, the seam going up to be lost in the dark lace that bound each leg. I swallowed. There must be some atavistic trigger that makes the sight of a garter fastened to the top of a stocking rouse a primitive hunting instinct. It's like a crosshairs laid over a particularly delectable prey. Almost irresistible.

The straps of each garter climbed the curves of her ass, one on each side, neatly framing the beautiful cleft between two graceful hemispheres. Her skin shone silvery pale, and again I flexed my fingers. Then I saw the dark fishtail shape of a lace thong flowing from the top of her ass over each hip and disappearing under the garter belt.

I frowned.

"Little One, was I mistaken in the purpose of your invitation?"

She turned her head over her shoulder, eyes surprised. This wasn't how the script in her head was written. "Um...what?" she murmured, and then caught herself, maintaining her demeanor. "What do you mean, Sir?" She looked confused, a little lost, and my heart beat a little faster at the adorably sweet expression.

I stepped closer behind her, deliberately, keeping my face

stern as I met her eyes. "I asked"—my hand went to her neck, caressing the smooth skin there—"if I was mistaken"—fingers curled up into her hair—"as to why"—tightened, her breath hissing as my fist clenched, tilting her head up and toward me—"you invited me here."

My face was centimeters from hers, and I could feel the warm skin of her ass pressed against my trousers, her skirt still held up in tight shaking fists. She knew I wasn't actually upset—the swell of my cock pressing through my trousers against her buttocks was evidence of that. However, arousal did not translate into kindness in our particular dynamic. In fact, it often resulted in the opposite. She knew that. I felt her tense with fearful anticipation and grind her ass against me in spite of it. Because of it.

"You asked me to come here and take you," I growled, my eyes locked on hers. "You were quite specific about your desire for fucking and sucking and beating and kneeling and having me, for lack of a more convenient term"—I tightened my grip slightly—"fuck your shit up." Her pupils dilated slightly with the added rush of endorphins.

"Yes, Sir..." she breathed out, an eager, trembling sound.

"And I, in turn, was quite specific as to the manner in which you were to present yourself."

"I thought...that is, I mean, I did, Sir, I thought..." I could see her mind racing, comparing the inventory of what she was wearing with the emails and chats we'd exchanged, the many flirtations that had led to this evening. I knew she would go over and over them in her mind, looking for something she'd missed or added, round and round in her head, and I let her wheels spin.

The fact was that she was perfect. She was wearing exactly what I'd requested, from the long skirt to the thin white cotton blouse. Heels to hair and everything in between, lovely and luscious and a feast for my eyes to savor.

But beauty is only part of this kind of play. The spice comes from the fear and the sweet dissonance of conflicting desires, to please and to be punished.

My part was, in effect, to season the experience. To taste.

"It's not the 'what,' Little One. It's the 'how.' Do you recall my views on the proper deportment of thong and garter belt?"

"Yes, Sir...you prefer the thong over the garter belt."

"Yes, Little One, that's what I said. And you responded with a very particular statement, one that I never forgot." I turned her head slightly so that my warm breath tickled her sensitive ear. "You said you'd never had occasion to dress in such a slutty way."

She didn't reply, but I felt her body react to the words.

"So I'm forced to wonder if perhaps I was misled as to the nature of this occasion. Perhaps you don't want to be on your knees. To feel my cock fill your throat till you gasp but still want it deeper. That sopping cunt of yours slam-fucked till you can barely walk, forced to cum for me till you're hoarse and still beg for more." I made the words guttural, growling, letting the monosyllables strike her desire with physical force. She was grinding against me harder now, and it took every bit of resolve I had not to push back.

But no, I was a rock of will upon which her growing lust crashed, and I continued. "That's how I remember our conversation. That's what I thought you invited me for." I hissed angrily in her ear. "Was I wrong?"

She whimpered softly. "No..."

"Then say it. Tell me what you want."

"I...I want you, Sir."

"That's all? Simple enough. I'm here." I tightened my fingers again, eliciting another soft, high moan. "Your ass says you want more. Tell me what you want, Little One."

She made another keening sound, and I shook her slightly. "Tell me!"

"I...I want you to...to fuck me, Sir." Suddenly the barrier was broken, and the words poured out in a rush. "I want to taste you...I...I want to suck you hard and cum on your hard... c—" She paused for a moment, and I thought I might have to pull the word out of her, but then she swallowed, licked her lips, and forced it out. "Your...c-*cock* over and over and feel your hand on me, in me, taking me, I want you to take me, Sir, use me..." Her tongue darted out to wet her lips again, and one more word whispered out. "Hard."

I kept my grip painfully tight, but I let my lips softly brush her ear, enjoying the tremble of her body. "That's good to hear, Little One." I felt her relax slightly, thinking the immediate danger had passed.

I brought my other hand up, across her body, knowing the upward tilt of her head would keep her from seeing what I held there. When the knife was near her opposite ear I pressed the release, letting the solid metallic click carry over her panting breath. She rewarded me with a low moan as her body tensed against mine. "But first, you must atone."

I let the tip of the blade prick her earlobe, then rest against the hollow just behind her ear. "It will hurt, Little One." She was frozen in a rictus of pleasure and fear as the sharp steel traced a line down her neck, across her collarbone and down the V of her blouse. "You will suffer. For your transgression." I kissed her ear again, lightly. "For me."

For a moment I was tempted to cut away each button of her blouse, visions of binding her in ragged strips of ruined cotton filling my head...but no, this was to be savored, and knowing that her hands would be unbuttoning them for me was a far sweeter anticipation. When the blade met the fabric I lifted it from her skin, letting the point bounce up and lightly press in at the upper swell of each breast.

"But I promise you, Little One, your atonement will be worth it." Over the left nipple, drawing it down her ribs not hard enough to cut the fabric or even hurt. I was simply communicating the potential for either consequence with the pressure through the fabric against her skin.

"In the end..." Lower, I pushed the tip into the hollow of her hip for a moment. Finally I laid the flat of the blade directly against her mons. "You will thank me."

She pressed forward against it, involuntarily, and stopped only as she realized the tip of the knife was poised directly over her clit. Protected by fabric or not, that was enough to make her freeze again. Her body felt electric, senses awake and craving more stimulation, a sweet antinomy of the need to move and the thrill of fear.

I used my grip on her hair—such a useful tool, the head, when it comes to making bodies do what you want—to bend her forward slightly, and her hands came up instinctively on either side of the door frame, just as I knew they would. Her lower body couldn't move against the knife, forcing her to lean forward, thrusting her ass out nicely, making a little shelf where the bunched fabric of her skirt stayed as I finally released her hair, withdrew the knife and stepped back.

This was the moment to savor, the *pièce de résistance.* I took in the sweet sight as she held herself open, exposed, waiting for me, legs stretched long and taut by the fuck-me stilettos, stockings and garters and thong and belt wrapping her ass like the best fucking birthday present of my life.

The adrenaline coursed through my blood as well, heightening every sense, letting me appreciate the subtle, tiny factors of each second in high-resolution surround-sound sensation. I stored each memory for later even as my hands moved, quickly pulling the thong away from the top of her ass, my knife flashing, slicing up and down the fabric on either side. The sharp blade sliced the *Agent Provocateur* lace with no thought to expense. *Shouldn't've provoked me.* It was a barrier to the way I wanted things, which made it mine to destroy. That was the magical gift she was giving me, this tiny bubble of time when everything was according to my will.

As I carefully put the knife away with one hand, I pulled down sharply on the thong with the other. It slid from under the garter belt and between her legs with a grudging snap of elastic. The friction forced her hips back farther, and she spread her feet for balance. I took advantage of the opportunity and thrust my hand, still holding the ruined thong, between her legs, cupping her vulva and almost lifting her. I could feel the heat and wet through her panties. I reveled in the dulcet music of her voice crying out with desire and, I suspected, frustrated loss at the expensive atonement. Still she pressed down against my hand, grinding, arching her back.

"I love hearing your cries, Little One." I lifted the thong, now soaked with her own juices, to her face, letting the fabric fall against her, knowing she could smell and taste the lust that filled her body. I reached up with my other hand, pulling it into a tight band against her throat for a moment, letting the collared and choked sensation fill her mind with implications...then up farther, along the soft skin of her neck and chin, forcing the fabric past her lips, pulling harder, letting it bite into the edges of her mouth, letting her tongue taste the sharp tangy sweetness of her cunt. Her eyes grew a bit wider, and I knew that her pussy would be throbbing harder at the thought of the gag.

I chuckled soft and low. "Oh, no, Little One, if I want that sweet mouth filled, I have far better things to shove into it."

To prove the point I lifted the cloth out of her mouth, suddenly, and covered her lips with mine, filling her mouth with the devouring release of my own desire. I poured all of my own pent-up pulsating need into that kiss, letting the world, our bodies, everything fall away as our tongues danced to the music of our longing, our sex, our urgent need.

I let it build, let it grow between us until I could feel every nerve quivering with exquisite tension.

Then I stepped away. Stepped back around, directly behind her again, matter-of-factly tying the thong around her eyes, knowing that the humiliation and hotness of the act would compensate for any inadequacies in its actually impeding her sight.

As I lifted my hand high, I took one final look at the smooth, exposed skin of her ass, creamy white and unblemished, taut and offered before me. Final, because the night would bring color to those cheeks, first the red of the spanking, then the darker welts of the cane, the stripes of my belt as she twisted and writhed in the ropes to come. That skin would become slick with lube as I fucked her, with her own juices as my fist inside of her made her squirt and scream and cum again and again. My own creamy whiteness would be shot across that beautiful ass as she offered it to me with a whispered *"Please, Sir, fuck me,"* through lips thick and swollen from sucking my cock.

But all of that was yet to come. Now, for just this savored moment, her ass was pristine, a trembling, sacrificial offering by a supplicant at the temple of power and lust. How fortunate was I to be chosen by her to fulfill the role of cruel celebrant?

I let my hand fall with all of the joyful weight of that responsibility. The strike of my hand on her flesh made a sharp, solid cracking sound. I saw the wave of pleasure roll through her as her attenuated senses were overwhelmed by the blow.

The first of many, but before I could continue, she filled the silence with the simplest and sweetest words a dominant man can hear:

"Thank you, Sir."

I paused. "You're welcome, Little One."

My hand fell.

DAY JOB

Deborah Castellano

She had long since stopped thinking he would ever notice her. To be fair, he didn't seem to notice much of anyone or anything outside of his books. His lectures were always well attended, the few times he gave them, but he never seemed to notice the disproportionate amount of women attending, for his field. Even after working for him for several blissful years, she had never observed so much as a phone call or email from a girlfriend or a wife, so it wasn't as if he noticed women outside the workplace, either.

It was a puzzle she diligently worked at. Her work was always completed early and to perfection. She always made sure she looked her best with her nails perfectly done, her hair arranged just so and her Benefit's Espionage lipstick flawlessly applied. It didn't seem to matter whether she brought candied ginger scones, tiny organic blueberry muffins or madeleines dipped carefully in dark chocolate. He certainly never seemed aware that they came from her kitchen. His tea service was always laid out exactly at three o'clock, everything polished to perfection. Every month, she chose a different imported tea: Heritage Ceylon Tea Blend No. 16, Formosa Silver Tip Oolong, Lapsang Souchong. She knew she should write a proper expense report but never could make herself do so.

He usually took tea alone in his office, poring over one worn leather-bound book or another in long since dead languages. The rest of the time, she would answer his phone, assist him in his research and organize his publications, which left her plenty of time to daydream about all of the terrible things she would do to him, if he just got the hint. She was generally good at being an engaging conversationalist, but something about being around him struck her with an inconvenient shyness. He was a quiet man, rarely speaking outside of dictation, which didn't help matters. He would occasionally gently reprimand her when something went awry despite her best efforts, or absent-mindedly say, *"Good girl,"* when she did something especially outstanding. She knew she should correct his saying that, but her heart beat so fast when he did, she could never bring herself to do so.

It was a cliché to be in love with your boss, but she didn't care. Not even when her girlfriends would tease her mercilessly over French Greyhounds at Zoe's, all of them leaving with their tiny purses full of email addresses and phone numbers.

She had to do something but she didn't know what. Get a new job? She shuddered at the thought. Set her sights on the other men constantly vying for her attention at cocktail parties and cafés? It never worked; it always came back to him.

Finally, on one of these outings, after she'd politely declined the third strange man's offer to refill her drink, her friend Grace had had enough. She tipsily pointed her finger at her and said, "Oh, for god's sake! Haven't you ever seen an old movie before?

The secretaries always dress sexy, act smart and have moxie. That's what you need! Moxie! Now go and get him!"

She spent the weekend pondering Grace's words, watching old movies, taking notes and drinking merlot. Grace was right; she needed a plan. Nothing she had done so far had gotten his attention; obviously more drastic measures were needed. And if he refused her, he might as well fire her anyway. She didn't know how much longer she could stand being in love with him and working for him, as it was.

Moxie, moxie, moxie. Just saying the word made her feel braver on Monday morning as she got to her desk. After Grace had pulled the plan out of her, she had insisted they go shopping for an added boost. Inspired by the old movies, they found a sexy, short, white pencil skirt with a black pin-dot print that accentuated her ample rump awesomely, and a short-sleeved, clingy black top with a sweetheart neckline that gave her hourglass figure extra oomph and showed off her buxom assets. After some coaxing and a quick cocktail stop, Grace pulled her into Frederick's of Hollywood for a black satin push-up bra, black ruffled panties, a black garter belt with red-ribbon suspenders and back-seamed stockings.

Now she nervously checked her watch and saw that he would be there in just a moment, so she took a deep breath and carefully climbed the small ladder in her kitten heels and pretended to look for a book. He walked in, looking down at his eReader intently, and sat at his desk. Her heart pounded and she felt like she couldn't breathe as she waited for him to look at her. Waited...and waited...

Instead of feeling discouraged or slinking back to her desk like she normally would, her new mantra had her feeling something else—annoyed. She deliberately dropped a book to the floor and he looked up at her, startled, as she had never dropped anything before. Feeling a surge of anger, she deliberately met his gaze and slowly dropped another book on the floor. And then another. And then another. He kept her gaze, saying nothing. She climbed down the ladder furiously and headed toward her desk, writing her resignation in her head while mentally going through a list of who she would call first to take her out tonight to assuage her ego. She hadn't noticed him standing up until she was almost on top of him. She brushed past him and found herself caught by the hair. Using her hair as a leash, he pulled her closer. Her pulse quickened, even as she crossed her arms and glared.

"Don't you think there are other ways to get my attention?" he asked softly.

"Yes, yes I do! But none of them have worked so far."

"It would have been unprofessional for me to have done anything without first being certain of your feelings."

Twisting herself around, she looked him square in the eye and found herself saying slowly and deliberately, "Fuck. Professionalism."

He couldn't hide his smile or the way his eyes lit up. He cleared his throat. "Are you implying that you are interested in a romantic *and* working relationship with me?"

"Yes," she said quietly, "I am."

"Excellent," he said. "Kneel."

"Sir?"

"Now."

Biting her lip, she knelt down on the floor, unable to breathe, form words or thoughts—anything. Bowing her head slightly, she tried to focus on the pattern swirling on the dark auburn carpet while she listened to him pace around her with the slow thoughtful steps he took when thinking about some perplexing problem. The longer he paced, the more she tried to make herself breathe in a normal, orderly fashion, and the more she failed at getting even a short, shallow breath out.

Eventually, he sat down in the big leather chair behind his old-fashioned wooden desk. She felt the weight of his stare upon her and cautiously looked up.

"You have apparently made it your life's goal to torment me."

"No, Sir, I..."

"I have not given you permission to speak." He spoke in the same calm, measured tones that he always used with her. Obediently, she became quiet and chewed the inside of her cheek.

"You are to crawl over to me on your hands and knees. You will then lean over my desk, and I will attempt to instill a better work ethic in you."

Everything felt calm inside her as she crawled over to him with her head held high and managed to go from her crouched position to standing in a reasonably graceful manner. Draping herself over his desk, she closed her eyes and waited.

"You will repeat after me: 'I will not drop books.'"

"I will..." There was a whoosh of air and then his hand on her bottom. She let out a startled cry.

"Pay attention, please."

"I will not drop books." Every ragged word that came out of her mouth was punctuated by a solid whack to her bottom.

"Again."

"I will not drop books!"

"Again."

"I will not drop books!"

"Good girl. Now lock the door and take your clothes off for me, I want to see what you're wearing underneath."

Shaking, she moved from the desk, her ass still smarting delightfully as she locked the door. Being ordered to take off her clothes added to her excitement. She didn't even feel anxious about it; after all, she was doing what she was told. She slowly unzipped her skirt and stepped out of it, still wearing her stockings and heels, and then pulled her top over her head and dropped it beside her. Normally, she would feel a little self-conscious about her zaftig figure when taking off her clothes, but now she didn't feel anything but glorious.

He moved to where she stood and his hands moved over her, gently running over her back and then stroking her full ass. He stroked the back of her legs, lingering again over her ass, and then stroked her rounded tummy moving up to her satin-clad breasts, plucking at her nipples slightly and then more firmly, making her gasp.

"You have the most amazing body," he murmured in her ear.

She shivered. "Thank you, Sir."

"Take your panties off, please."

Unable to think straight, she nervously wobbled over to the desk and used it for balance to carefully shimmy out of her panties.

Regaining his grasp from earlier, he pulled her hair from the base of her neck, making her feel even more flushed than before. His other hand gently stroked her stocking-clad thighs, moving slowly but surely higher. It was impossible to hide how he made her feel and out of habit, she tried to move slightly away from him.

"I haven't told you to move, small one."

She nodded, taking a breath as she tried to still herself. She bit her lip hard, so she wouldn't moan too loudly when his hand moved to caress her glistening mound. His fingers softly circled her clit making it so she couldn't help but arch her back slightly and move against his hand. When she leaned back, she tried

to suppress a gasp when she felt the weight of his hard cock
pushing against his pants.

"Tell me what you want."

"You," she said simply, breathing hard.

"How?" he asked, softly in her ear. She shuddered.

"I...want you inside me."

He stroked her some more and made a soft purring noise.
"Oh?"

"Yes. Please. Please, Sir." Desperate for him, she no longer
cared how she sounded. "I need you."

"And I burn for you, my dear ."

She heard him unzip his pants and felt his cock against her.
Unable to stop herself from pressing back against him, she felt
her body humming with eagerness to have him inside her. He
continued to stroke her clit in measured, thoughtful circles,
while he entered her slowly and began thrusting. Tugging at
her hair firmly, he forced her to expose her neck to him. She
couldn't help herself: she cried out again and again, pushing
back against him, clutching urgently at the desk. Wave after
wave of pleasure washed over her body as she gasped, a fine
sheen of sweat glistening on her back. Time ceased to exist in
any meaningful way for her, blissed out as she was. Eventually
she heard his voice in her ear, soft and rough.

"What do you want, little one?"

"I...want to please you."

"You already do," he said sweetly, circling his hips against
her.

She moaned incoherently.

"I want to feel your release. Please," she managed to get out.

His breathing hitched and he pulled her close to him, pounding
against her. Limp as a kitten, she was unable to do anything but
feel him move inside her. But her excitement mounted as she felt

him coming closer to his climax. Pushing back against him in time with his thrusts, all she could do was gasp, her voice gone now. With a sigh, he came inside her. He gently kissed her neck and straightened her clothes.

"I'll expect tea as usual at three, please. Be ready for me to take you to dinner at seven. Have you brought those lovely scones you bake?"

STAND HERE

Nym Nix

S tand here," she says, leading me to a leather armchair in the corner. The room is softly lit. I see the flocked wallpaper, mahogany bed and, beside the chair, a side table with an ice bucket, a decanter of something amber and a crystal glass. Then she puts the blindfold over my eyes.

I put my gloved hands behind my back and wait. The door snicks closed. I bow my head. The silence of the room washes over my bare skin, leaving it tingling. The minutes stretch out. The dark begins to play havoc with my equilibrium. I feel myself sway, my feet working to find balance on the teetering heels of my stilettos. Finally, I hear the murmur of voices from the corridor. I take a quick breath and adjust my posture. I pull back my shoulders and suck in my stomach, but I keep my head bowed and my arms relaxed. I want to make a good impression. There is the sound of the door opening.

"Here you are, Sir," she says. "Please, just ring if there's anything more you need."

"Thank you."

His voice is quiet. I hear the door close. There is a soft sound, as though he is taking off a jacket, and then more quiet noises as he moves about the room. I wonder what he's like. There was not enough in those two words to tell me whether he is old or young, large or small. Only that he is male.

Nothing happens. I hear small sounds, as though he is fussing about the room. *Is he looking at me?* My heart is pounding, but I try to breathe quietly. I try to calm myself by counting, but with each second that passes, my anxiety grows. *Have I done something wrong?*

Every time I book a session at this club, there are the same questions. Will there be much pain? How will I be tested? Will I find someone...? I have been reprimanded, scolded, schooled, whispered to, shouted at, reviled, praised, instructed, cosseted, used and discarded so many times. But never ignored. The disappointment of it rises in my throat, threatening to choke me. Tears suddenly fill my eyes.

First one, then another, track down my cheeks and creep along my jaw. I'm doing my best to control myself. If this keeps up, I will start to sniffle, and that will be humiliating. But stopping is harder to do than it is to think about, and the tears keep coming.

Eventually, well after I have lost track of time, there is a creak of leather as he sits, followed by the crystal chink of ice dropping into a glass. Moments later I hear the delicate gurgle of liquid being poured.

"You have been very patient," he says, his voice still quiet. It is hard to read. Is he pleased? I could have sworn there was a note of uncertainty there. Some of them like a little rebellion. If that's what he wants, I suspect I've failed on that count. The tear-tracks on my cheeks burn coolly.

"Thank you, Sir," I whisper.

"Come here," he says. "Sit on my lap."

Nervously I sidestep where the small table is—or where I think it is. I'm clumsy from standing still for so long, and I brush the side of it with my thigh, setting the ice tinkling madly. I know I'm there when my knee bumps his. I turn, and as I go to sit down, he puts his hand on the back of my thigh.

"Stop," he says. I freeze, about to sit. His hands explore the dent in my thigh where my stocking clings. He slides a finger in between the elastic and my skin and tracks it around to the soft flesh between my legs. I feel his knuckle graze the lower curve of my arse and I feel a finger brush over the pursed lips of my labia. All of a sudden I am all over goose bumps. He extracts his finger, the elastic snapping back gently, and follows the cleft between my buttcheeks up, up.

I have almost stopped breathing at this point. In the silence I hear the sounds of his breath as it begins to speed up. I almost begin weeping again from relief.

His hands move upward, roving over my back. He reaches around my rib cage and pulls me down onto him. Immediately I am aware of the hard rod of his erection digging into my left buttock. He runs his hands briefly over my belly, before sliding them up to cup my breasts. By now my nipples are hard and taut, and he makes a little rumble of satisfaction in his chest as his fingers find them. My heart is beating faster again.

"Turn to the side," he instructs, and I shift myself on his lap. One hand stays with one of my breasts, his fingers acquainting themselves with my nipple in exquisite detail, while the other hand tracks up over my collarbone to my throat. When he reaches my jaw he pauses, cupping my face in both hands, turning it toward him, pushing my chin up. His thumbs run over the last vestiges of my tears, smearing them away.

"Why are you crying?" he asks. There is a new, harsh note to his voice. He almost sounds angry.

"I—I'm sorry, Sir," I whisper. "I thought you didn't like me. You ignored me for so long." He utters a short bark of laughter.

"Really."

He pushes a thumb into my mouth, depressing my tongue. I quiver. His skin is rough and tastes faintly salty. He runs his other hand down my body, stopping to toy roughly with my other nipple, before sliding over my belly and between my legs. His fingers—as rough as his thumb—push between the lips of my sex and thrust deep into my pussy. It's brutal, but pretty soon I am gasping around the obstruction of his thumb.

Then he stops.

I can't help the whimper that escapes my lips.

"Now, we're going to play a game," he says into my ear. I nod once. I can't speak with his thumb in my mouth. He extracts it, but then puts the fingers of his other hand into my mouth—the ones that have just been inside me.

"Lick them clean," he says. My mouth and nose are filled with the scent of me, and my arousal.

"Good girl," he says when he's satisfied. I could squirm with pleasure. I can feel his hard-on pressing emphatically into my thigh. He removes his hand and shifts around. It feels like he's trying to dig something out of his pocket. I wait in darkness, feeling the comfort of his other hand resting possessively on my hip.

There is a muffled jingle. Then whatever he is trying to get at is extracted, and the tinny jingle becomes clear.

"On the floor," he says. "Let's see how clever you are."

I slide off his lap and kneel between his legs on the floor. The carpet is thick and plush against my hands. One of his hands dances over my shoulder, takes hold of my chin and tilts my face up. His fingers trace my jaw and my lips. Then he slides his hand behind my neck, takes hold of my hair and twists it into a rope. My breath comes short and my body tenses up. It doesn't hurt, but the suggestion of pain is more than enough to set my pulse racing...again. My sex is still throbbing.

"Okay, sweetheart," he says into my ear. "I want you to find this." He jingles the thing hard in my ear.

"I'm going to count. You have thirty seconds."

I feel him lean past me. I feel the movement of his body as he rolls the thing across the floor. I listen for the jingle as it careens merrily away from me. There is another abrupt jangle as it hits something, bounces and then stops still. He is still holding my hair tight in his fist.

"Hands and knees," he instructs. "Pick it up in your mouth. Thirty seconds. Go." He releases me. I scamper forward. I'm aware of how I must look. Then, a moment later, I hear a new sound. I freeze, listening. There it is again. It sounds like he's pressing buttons on a mobile phone. He's not watching. He might not even really be counting.

Deflated, I lurch forward, feeling with my hands, but not really thinking about anything but this dom's lack of interest. And crack my head on something hard. I gasp, sitting back on my heels, my hand on top of my head.

"You okay?" he asks. Numbly, I nod. There is a silence.

"Use words," he snaps.

"Yes, Sir," I mumble. "I'm okay."

"Fifteen seconds."

I put my hands out and feel the footboard of the bed. I feel for the leg and then around on the carpet for the damn jingly thing. It's not there. I feel my way along to the other side. There, a foot away from the other leg, I find a small plastic ball. It's got holes all over it, and when my fingers first nudge it, it jingles. I lower my upper half to the floor to where I can grab it in my mouth then crawl back to where he is sitting.

"Drop it in my lap," he murmurs, as though distracted by something else. I do as I'm told. There is a moment of silence.

"Thirty-seven," he says. "Too long." All of a sudden I'm on tenterhooks again.

"Bring me the crop," he says. "Do you know where it is?"

I nod then remember he doesn't like silence.

"Yes, Sir," I say.

"Good girl." With a little curl of pleasure, I hear the smile in his voice.

I crawl over to the foot of the bed, and then go from there to the dresser where the toys are kept. The crop is a popular one, so it's kept in the top drawer. I take it out and crawl back to him with it between my teeth. When I'm back at his feet he touches my hair and runs his fingers down the side of my face. They stop to rest on the crop, and he tugs it from my grip.

He hooks a finger into my mouth.

"Over to the bed," he says, standing up.

I expect him to lead me, but actually it's as though he's letting me lead him, testing me to see if I remember where the bed is.

I remember. My head is still throbbing.

At the bed, he twists up my hair again and draws me up, then pushes me forward and down. I am pressed face-first into the duvet, its crisp coolness sharp against my skin. He pauses to caress me once again. I like this about him. His hands are constantly roving over me, finding me out. He runs his hands over the skin of my arse and down to touch the lips of my sex once more. They are still slick and sensitized. He murmurs under his breath. Then he puts one hand in the center of my back, and I feel him lay the crop against the top of my thighs.

"Seven strokes."

I shiver. "Yes, Sir," I say into the thickness of the duvet.

He brings the crop down. I jump and try not to cry out. He moves his hand from my back and slides it into my hair. He pulls my head back.

"Come on, kitten," he says. "I want to hear you."

"Oh!" I mew out. I can feel the sting from where he struck, and he's pulling my hair hard this time. It comes down again, and again. I cry out with each blow, but I want more. I spread my legs and thrust my arse up into the air, and this time the tag of the crop catches the tender skin on the inside of my thigh.

I yowl.

By the time he's done, my face is wet with tears again. I slide off the bed into a puddle of misery and elation at his feet. I feel him kneel down in front of me and he takes my chin in his hands, turning my face up.

"That was lovely," he murmurs, smudging his thumbs through my tears. His fingers brush over the lump on my forehead. "You need to be more careful." Something inside me ignites. If he directed me to crawl over hot coals right now, I'd do it.

"Okay, let's try again, kitten," he says. There's a jingle as he picks up the cat toy again. "Listen carefully." I feel the movement and hear a sharp jangle as he throws it. I hear it bounce three times and then roll slowly to a stop. I turn my head blindly, trying to judge the direction. He puts his hand against my throat.

"Thirty seconds," he says. "Go."

This time I crawl a little more carefully. Certain kinds of pain, yes. My arse is tingling in a way that makes my toes curl. But I'm not keen to court a concussion. I find the cat toy on the other side of the dresser.

My finger bumps against it, and it lets out one clear chime. I freeze. Has it been thirty seconds?

"Twenty seconds," he says, as if reading my mind. Sadly I pick up the ball in my mouth and crawl back to the bed. I feel my way to where he's sitting and drop it into his lap.

"Did you cheat?" he asks coldly.

"No, Sir!" I cry.

"Did you look?" His voice is implacable.

"No, Sir," I whisper.

"How can I trust you?" he asks me.

"Please, Sir," I say, hesitating. "Perhaps I should have a stroke for each second under thirty. You did say thirty seconds."

"I did," he sounds pleased now. "Good girl. Over my knee, I think." Trembling with anticipation I stand up. He takes my wrists in one hand and pulls me over his lap. He starts by putting one hand between my shoulder blades and gently running his other hand over my arse. There are tender parts from where he used the crop. I moan. It's always worse when they start off gentle. He moves his hand, and I brace for the impact. But instead he reaches lower and nudges my thighs apart. He strokes my labia once, twice, then gently slides a finger just inside. I moan again as he pulls his finger away. I want him so badly now.

When his hand slams down on my arse, I squeak. He spanks me again and again. My buttcheeks must be glowing red. I've lost count of how many times he's hit me. Far more than I purportedly earned. I squirm on his lap as he rests his hand on the heated skin of my arse between blows, and the hand between my shoulder blades pushes down harder.

"Please!" I sob. "Please, Sir!" But I don't know what I'm asking for. He keeps going. His hand is hard and leathery. I can't even hear the sound of it striking my skin now—the blood is pounding in my ears and I'm sobbing out loud.

Eventually he stops. But I don't get any sort of respite. For at that point he starts finger-fucking me all over again. I'm squirming, I can't help it. He pulls out and slaps me sharply, and I cry out. But when he thrusts back in I begin squirming all over again. It is so good.

He gives up. I moan as he withdraws his hand. Then he has hold of my hair once more and drags me off his lap.

"This is not acceptable," he growls into my ear. Tearfully I try to nod. His grip on my hair is tight.

"No, Sir. I'm sorry, Sir," I whimper.

"Get up," he says, pulling my hair. I stagger up.

"On your back. Spread your legs."

I obey. My sex is throbbing and running wet. He runs his hands up the outside of my thighs to my hips. He drags me closer to the edge of the bed. His hands fumble for my breasts. He grips them too, bending over me to tease at the points with his teeth until I cry out. Then his fingers are inside me once more. I concentrate hard on pulling my legs back, opening myself up for him, trying not to writhe.

"Good girl," he says. "Now don't you dare come until I tell you to."

Bastard. With that phrase, I'm there. Teetering on the edge, and he hasn't even touched my clit.

"Please, Sir," I beg. "Please let me come!"

"No," he snaps, and starts to thumb my clit. I groan and sob, but he's implacable.

"Please, Sir!" I wail. "Please, fuck me!"

He lets go of me entirely. I am hanging in a silence broken only by my own ragged breath. Then I hear the magic sound. The sound of his fly.

"Say it again," he whispers.

"Please fuck me, Sir!" I gasp. "Please, please let me come."

He grabs my legs and hauls me close, impaling me on his cock.

"Don't you come," he says, slamming into me hard. I cry out, incoherent now. He's holding my knees so wide I'm afraid I'll snap. I can feel him getting harder and bigger with every thrust. I'm gritting my teeth and yelling through them, trying not to come. He's pounding himself against the wall of my womb, and every fiber of my body wants to explode.

"Now," he grunts. "Frig yourself. Come for me, kitten."

I reach down and begin to rub. He begins to grunt with every thrust. Then I'm yelling, arching myself up into him, and he's coming with a guttural roar.

Afterward he leans over me, pressing his forehead on mine, running a finger along my jaw and between my lips.

"A good start," he says. "Do you think you'd like to see me again?" My heart leaps.

"Yes, Sir. Please, Sir, I'd like that," I whisper.

"Sit up," he says. "Clean me up."

I kneel at his feet and clean his drooping cock with my tongue. I can taste him and me together. When I'm done, I draw up his briefs, zip his fly and buckle his belt. There is the sound of fabric moving over skin, and something soft drops onto my shoulders.

"Here," he says, his voice gentle. "Put that on." His shirt. He tugs it over my breasts. I want to melt. But a small part of me quivers in excitement. Does that mean he's not finished with me?

"Bring me the phone."

I feel my way to the bedside table and find the phone. From the sound of it, he's gone back to the armchair, so I crawl awkwardly over, cradling the phone against my breasts. I kneel at his feet.

His fingers bump mine as he takes the phone. I hear the click of buttons and the tickle of a voice as reception answers.

"Hi," he says. "It's room twelve. Can you bring up Henley, please?" His voice is calm and courteous. He strokes my hair and cups my chin.

"There's someone I want you to meet."

My stomach does a little flip-flop. *What does that mean?* Another dom? Another sub? A partner?

There is a knock on the door.

"Enter," he says.

"Here you go, Sir," says a female voice.

"Henley," he says, his voice firm with command. "Come here." There is the shuffle of a loping gait on carpet, and the huff-huff of canine breath. I freeze. This was not a box I ticked.

"Thank you," he says, and the door clicks shut. I'm close to panic.

"Henley, sit," he says. He takes up my resisting hands and strips off the black, satin gloves. The air is cool on my fingers. I shiver, my skin gone to gooseflesh again. Holding my wrists, he stretches out my arms. I pull back, but his grip is insistent. I hear the dog close his mouth and sniff at me, and his cold nose touches a fingertip. I recoil. But the dom grips my wrists tighter.

"What do you think, Henley?" he asks. He sinks my fingers into the dog's thick fur. It is soft and coarse, but not long. And the dog is big. A Labrador or golden retriever, perhaps? The dog pants calmly, his warm breath fanning my face. Despite myself, I stroke him. My fingers find the straps of some sort of harness. My stomach does another flip-flop. I explore further. Lying over the dog's back is a rigid handle.

"He's...!" I gasp.

"My guide dog," says the dom.

I continue to run my hands over the dog's harness, in something of a daze.

"Do you still think you'd like to see me again?" he asks. His voice is carefully neutral. A vision starts forming in my mind. Me on my hands and knees, strapped into a similar harness. Perhaps one with a bit. This dom's hands at the reins. My eyes at his service, along with the rest of my body.

"Oh yes, Sir," I beg. "Please, Sir."

DIRTY PICTURES

Thomas S. Roche

When Amy got home about six, a dirty picture waited for her on the kitchen table. Spotting it instantly, she walked over and picked it up without even bothering to turn on the overhead light. Dappled by the kitchen curtains, the dying light of the early evening illuminated a photo of a nude woman kneeling on a carpeted floor, wearing fishnet stockings and a black leather collar. Her nipples bore clamps with a shiny chain between them. Her face, downturned, bore a blankly submissive expression.

The woman was a pale brunette, like Amy, although this bitch looked young enough that she probably didn't need Miss Clairol to contend with occasional whispers of gray. That annoyed Amy; why were the goddamn women in porn always twenty years old?

The photo was shot up close, from not far above the ground. The woman's knees, far apart, revealed a shaved sex and a piercing through her clit. The woman's hands rested spread-fingered on her thighs. Her ass did not rest on her high heels, which were black and spiked. They were just visible between her open thighs, with an inch or so of clearance between heels and butt. It was so clearly a posture of submission, and at certain other times in certain other contexts, she would have gotten instantly and fiercely aroused looking at it. In bed, for instance, on Ev's laptop...or in a furtive moment at work when she was procrastinating.

But it had been a long commute, and Amy was not in a very good mood. She frowned. The colors were garish and the paper slightly shiny. The picture had clearly been printed from the high-quality color laser that Ev just *had* to have, to the tune of six hundred dollars that Amy, at the time, would have been just as happy not spending. For a moment, she was more pissed off than ever that her husband had insisted on the expenditure.

Then, as her eyes adjusted to the half-light, she read the note that Ev had penned above the centered photo on the printer paper. He'd written it in strict and unfamiliar capitals, much harsher than the usual script he used for notes to her.

YOU'VE BEEN A VERY BAD GIRL.

Amy took a breath. Her commute and her workday, the cost of the printer...it all melted away. Down at the bottom, underneath the dirty photo, Ev had written something else:

7:30.

Amy's heart pounded a little; it fluttered. She felt an unexpected tingling sensation go through her whole body. The sensation was midway between a chill and a fever. It wasn't very romantic; it felt like she'd just gotten food poisoning.

It didn't last long. The unpleasant sensation of panic rolled through her body quickly, never quite engaging her mind. But when it was gone, she felt like very little remained in her mind. She felt clear, calm, at peace...or maybe just so terrified that her brain had shut down.

With a glance at the kitchen clock, Amy started down the hall toward the bedroom. She unbuttoned her blouse as she went.

7:30. 7:30. 7:30. She turned it over and over again in her head as she stripped off her blouse, skirt, bra. She kicked off her shoes and pulled down her stay-ups—lace-topped but *nude*...sure as hell not *fishnet*. The fishnets, she kept in a special drawer...with the collar and the clamps and the...*other* things.

Amy didn't need to question what the *7:30* meant. She knew how her husband's mind worked. For some years she'd known how to shorthand his grunts and his shrugs and his stern looks of disapproval. They might have annoyed her, but she could translate them. A few months ago, when they started this full-time thing...as in, *all the time, 24/7, even when you sleep,* Amy had discovered a curious phenomenon about her own sexuality. Her monosyllabic husband had become a monosyllabic master...and it didn't bug her at all.

What *7:30* meant, she knew, was *Look like this by 7:30, slave.* What it meant was *When I come home, this is who you will be for me, no questions asked.* It meant, *Not only isn't this command open to negotiation, I won't even bother to tell you what to do. You will anticipate my needs based on fragmentary data, and god have mercy on your ass if you don't...because I, as your Master, will not.*

Amy was dripping like a faucet before she got in the shower. She had to spread her lips and direct the massager on her clit for a few minutes, just to calm down. The pleasure flowing through her body gentled her slightly; her heart rate slowed. She took deep breaths of steam.

She thought, *What will he want tonight?*

No answer could satisfy her. She had only to wait, and it

would all come to her. She had only to obey her Master's orders, and he would do with her as he pleased.

But she thought about it a lot. He wouldn't have chosen that picture if he hadn't wanted her *just like that*. On her knees, collared, tits clamped, legs spread...

The girl in the photo had clearly been a very bad girl. When the photo was taken, what was about to happen to her? Was she about to get spanked, whipped, caned?

Or was she just some stupid model, barely into her twenties, paid to put on a dog collar and tit clamps and fishnets and kneel there—nothing more?

Amy felt slightly perturbed again. She could never just let porn be porn. Closing in on forty, Amy always found herself annoyed that all of the women in the kind of porn she liked were so much younger than she was. She loved dirty pictures as much as Ev did. She loved looking at them herself...but she liked even better that it gave her Master ideas. Dirty ideas... *nasty* ones. All their best scenes had been inspired by dirty pictures.

As Amy's mind worked, she lost the sense of calm she'd felt briefly. As usual, she couldn't stop her brain from racing out of control. Why did her Master want her like the girl in the photo? What the hell had happened to her? Her mind swam with possibilities. The picture had imprinted itself in Amy's mind, but it gave very little indication of what her Master wanted from her tonight. Any dumb slut could throw on a cheap pair of fishnets and some $5 mail-order tit clamps and a $10.99 dog collar from Pet Parade and a Shoe Shack pair of high heels. Any stupid cunt could find herself kneeling and begging for attention. Had her stupid Master jerked his thing to a stupid college bitch who needed just a hundred dollars?

Or had the girl gotten what she needed? Had the girl in

the picture been spanked, whipped, caned, fingered, felt up, fucked?

Would *Amy* get fucked?

Trying to stop her racing mind, Amy got out of the shower, toweled dry and fucked with her hair a little. She'd managed not to get it too wet in the shower, so she let it go. When she dressed up for Ev—or dressed down, as in this case—she didn't spend much time on her hair. She'd learned long ago that her husband was all about the eyes—and, to a lesser extent, the lips. She could step away from her vanity sporting a freshly fucked atrocity of Medusa proportions on her head, and as long as she'd given her emerald peepers the drunk-crying-debutante treatment, she was the absolute essence of feminine beauty to Ev. If her lips were red-puckered like a streetwalker's kiss, then as far as Ev was concerned, she was a goddess.

Such knowledge, she'd found, came in handy for a wife. For a slave, it was absolutely invaluable.

Either way, it was good to have something to focus on. She painted her lips over and over again, till they veritably dripped, bright and red with a porn star-worthy pucker. She redid her eyes until they were as black-rimmed and nasty as a crying prom queen's.

It was 7:15, Amy suddenly realized. Ev was never late. His promptness, in fact, was legendary. It always annoyed the hell out of her—more so tonight than ever. She'd better haul ass.

Freshly painted, Amy pulled on her fishnets and stepped into the four-inch heels she'd worn, ironically enough, to their rehearsal dinner. She still couldn't walk in them, but she probably wouldn't be walking much.

She put her nipple clamps on, wincing. Then, with an air of ritual and reverence, Amy looked in the mirror and buckled her dog collar around her neck.

No, not a slave collar, she'd told Ev some time ago, back when this all was just a fantasy. *Not a fucking slave collar. That's so pretentious. If I were a slave, I'd want to be lower than a dog. I mean, that's why it's hot to wear a dog collar, right? Calling it a "slave collar" is just...ugh. It's for yuppies.*

When she delivered her little tirade, she was his girlfriend. Ev had found it amusing. Years later, as his wife, she asked to be collared. He had taken her to Pet Parade.

Had the girl in the picture gone to Pet Parade with her boyfriend, the way Amy had gone with Ev? Had her boyfriend felt her up in the aisle as he held each collar up to her neck, not caring who was watching—or maybe caring a little *too* much, knowing it made her wet to be shown off and embarrassed like that? Had the girl's barely postadolescent boyfriend cornered her in the parking garage and told her to lift her hair and show off her neck while he cut the price tag off her new collar with a jackknife...and then buckled it on her, right there in public, where anybody might have happened by and seen it? Had that happened to the naked-and-kneeling girl, the way it had happened to Amy?

Or was the girl in Ev's favorite fucking picture some pompous young goth who made trips to "the City" to buy a "slave collar" at some pretentious douche-bag shop named Dark Leather Master of Vampire Shadows Emporium or some fucking thing?

Even worse, maybe some sleazy porn producer just handed her a collar and barked, *Here, doll-face, put this on—collars are big this year.*

Amy took deep breaths, trying to stop her brain from spinning out of control. She walked down the hall to the kitchen. She took one last look at the picture on the table. *Bitch,* she thought about the girl in the picture, indulging in one last uncharitable thought as she wondered what Ev liked so much about her.

Amy tried to breathe deep and stay calm, feeling the pinch of the clamps on her nipples whenever her breath reached its deepest point.

Amy tried to memorize the kneeling girl's position.

She studied the picture till the kitchen clock said 7:28.

She went into the living room and dawdled for a desperate moment, trying to decide what the lighting should be. The sun was all the way down now, and the living room was far too dark to illuminate her properly. She wanted Ev to see her. She finally just turned on the torch lamp by the big picture window, and turned it down roughly halfway. The curtains were open. Standing in front of the window as she was, she'd be visible to the neighbors, if anyone bothered to look. She thought that was kind of hot...and in any event, she'd be down on her knees, very much out of anyone's line of sight...except her husband's.

Amy grabbed a throw pillow from the couch. It was way too slippery, and not wide enough to allow her to spread her knees as far as the girl in the picture, so she got rid of the throw and knelt on the hardwood.

I'll bag my fucking fishnets, she thought bitterly. She let it go.

She spread her knees wide. Her heart raced as she heard Ev's car in the driveway. She breathed slowly, forming a mental image of the girl in the dirty picture. She arched her back just so, put her hands on her thighs and lifted her ass above her heels. She shook her messy dark hair back over her shoulders to make sure that her tits were exposed. She looked down and tweaked her clamps a little, to make sure her tits looked symmetrical...or at least as symmetrical as possible.

She thought, *It's easy as hell to look good on camera when you're twenty and gravity hasn't had a crack at you.* When the collar came off in an hour, a few hours or tomorrow morning, she resolved to ask Ev what he liked about the girl. She resolved additionally to ask without a bitter bite to her tone.

Ev was mounting the stairs. Her husband's footsteps were heavy. She lowered her gaze submissively and spread her fingers across her thighs. With her legs all open like this, she could smell her sex. She smelled cunt-musky and shower-clean.

Ev's keys jangled in the lock. The door opened.

Master came in.

Amy fought the urge to look up at Ev. She kept her eyes down. Every second she did, she felt more submissive. Not being able to look up was torture, but it sent a hot shiver through Amy's body to hear Master's big, heavy feet on the hardwood floor as he neared her.

Finally, Master stood in front of her. He had something in his hand.

It was a big plastic bag marked CAMERA CONNEXION.

"Good evening, slave," said Ev.

"Good evening, Master," said Amy. She looked at the bag. It made her heart race.

Still holding the bag from Camera Connexion, Ev reached down and caressed her neck, then her tits. He toyed with her nipple clamps. Amy stayed still as she could, which wasn't very. She was turned on already, and Ev knew exactly where to touch her. He also knew how crazy it drove her to have him standing over her like this.

It didn't take long before Amy was in a froth, which had clearly been Ev's intention to begin with.

Without another word, he sat on the sofa behind Amy. Out of her sight, he fucked with the bag. Amy heard the click of his jackknife. She heard him slitting packages...boxes.

She heard the squeaking of Styrofoam and the tearing of paper and plastic. She heard the click as her Master fitted his new toy together. She resisted the urge to look back and see it.

Ev took his time. Amy's thighs began to ache, growing to a pleasant warmth as she struggled to hold her ass above the high heels and to keep her legs spread. It took effort to stay in the submissive position. The slow-building burn in her muscles sent a totally different sense of heat up inside her. She felt her cunt cooling, exposed to the air. She was really, really dripping.

"Did you like the picture?" her Master finally asked.

"It was hot," she said.

"The position or the girl?" he asked pointedly.

Amy felt her face turning red.

"I really liked the position," she said. Feeling suddenly guilty, she added, "And the girl's hot, too. She's gorgeous." It reddened her face to lie, but was it really a lie? The girl *was* hot. Amy was just a little bit of a jealous bitch. It wasn't the model's fault.

Behind her, Amy's Master said, "Eh." Something rippled at the back of her neck. After ten years of marriage, Amy knew psychically when her monosyllabic husband was shrugging.

And that was a shrug if she'd ever felt one.

"I'm sorry, Sir?" she said.

"I've always loved that picture," said Ev. "And the model's pretty...but you're so much hotter."

Amy's mouth opened. She couldn't say a word.

Ev's voice lowered, almost to a growl.

"But I still love the picture," he said. "I love how distressed she looks...and those clamps are tight. They must hurt like hell. If she's been kneeling like that for very long, I bet her ass and thighs must hurt." He said with a hint of sadistic pleasure: "Do yours?"

"Yes, Sir," said Amy. The burn from her buttocks pulsed into her sex.

Ev chuckled.

He got up off the couch and came toward her from behind. His big hand caressed Amy's shoulders. He reached down and teased her tits. Then he swept her long hair out of the way, so he could get a good angle on her breasts.

Towering over his wife, Ev aimed the camera. The camera's flash blinded Amy. She blinked, her eyes watering.

"Well, they're going to hurt a lot more before I'm through with you, slave," said Ev. "For years, I jerked off to pictures like that. And you ruined it, Amy. You're too fucking hot for your own fucking good. Or for *my* good. I finally decided, hell, they've got these great new full-featured DSLRs on deep discount. Why not go grab one?"

The flash came again. Amy blinked.

Evan spoke softly and cruelly.

"You've been a very naughty girl," he told Amy. "Screwing up my fantasy life like that. But you're going to make it right, aren't you? I'm gonna make you act out every single pose that ever got my dick hard." He chuckled. "Not all of them tonight, of course. But...tonight, we'll get a good start. Try to look sad, baby. Like you've just been kidnapped. Some madman's gonna do something *nasty* to you, Amy. Something dirty. You'll hate every minute of it, and the sick perv will get it all on camera. You're about star in the hottest fucking porno pictures anyone ever shot."

Three more flashes blinded Amy again in rapid succession. Tears filled her eyes. They spilled down her cheeks—slow tears, thick with mascara.

Ev said, "Oh yeah, yeah...I love that. Go ahead and cry like that. Perfect. Cry like you're scared."

So she did, and she was, even if that wasn't why she was crying. Evan caressed her all over and blinded her again and again and again.

As it turned out, the girl in the picture *did* have something very, very dirty done to her...and there was plenty more to come.

MY MASTER'S MARK

Lydia Hill

Hₒw are you with pain?"

I had to smile at the irony of the ink master's question.

"Trust me, I won't have a problem with the pain." After all, I'd been well trained to accept pain. Especially on the posterior, which was the area currently in question.

With a nod he escorted me into an enclosed area, seeing as how my ass would be exposed for all the world to see. Not that I had a problem with that, but perfect strangers might feel differently. Go figure.

I was preparing to get my first tattoo. He'd talked me through the process and I'd shown him the design concept and sample to draw from. I'd been mesmerized by the results he'd produced and now could not wait to see it blazing from my behind.

"A few minutes for prep, then we'll get started." My artist had been recommended by someone I commute with, a woman with stunningly lifelike tattoos, so I had great expectations for my own. I'd also spotted one of his female artists sporting the triskelion-style BDSM symbol, so I hoped my request wouldn't raise eyebrows.

I stripped off the black leather skirt, one I wore often for my Master, without an iota of self-consciousness. In the beginning of course, I'd blushed like a fool every time I was ordered to get naked. Now as I lay down on the table, I recognized that even the submissive act of exposing myself to this man had tripped my switch and that faint little buzz had begun to hum beneath my skin. I knew that familiar sensation.

Anticipation.

The ink master ran a razor over my ass and used some antibiotic wipes, and then he told me he was ready.

"Just say the word if at any point you need a break, or feel sick."

"I'll be fine. I promise."

The first touch of the needle on my flesh made me sigh. A sharp, hot sting, like a bee. At first it felt like what it was— a pointy invasion; but before long the sizzling pain began to spread, growing a bit more intense and diffuse. I started the slow descent that pain always brought.

I closed my eyes and recalled another time I'd bared my ass and accepted the pain. Master M's favorite torment was a long, hard spanking, and that day I'd asked him why.

"I beat your ass because I'm a sadistic bastard, that's why." His rough growl had heated me up as intently as his big hands were doing.

"I don't play those pussy games: 'naughty girl who needs a spanking' bullshit." He'd landed a few extra-hard whacks to punctuate his disdain. "I just like to watch your ass heat up and hear you beg me to stop."

I always did. Beg, I mean. He'd been pushing me since day one; urging me, bullying me beyond my preconceived notions of how much pain and torment I could take. Since the moment we met, he'd shown me I was far stronger than I'd thought and that my desire to please him allowed me to withstand almost anything he wanted to dole out.

Pain was Master M's thing, most assuredly. He truly was a sadist, but he was a full-service sadist. It wasn't just watching me moan through a paddling, or scream when he whaled on me with his big leather belt. There was no limit to the crude acts he'd demanded I perform. And I had come to crave every debasing moment at his hands and he knew it. The further he pushed me, the prouder I was to satisfy him.

The continued steady application of the tattoo needle kept the sensations ramping up. The endorphin glow had begun. The pain was throbbing now, the way it did when Master used his hand on the same spot, again and again until my muscles quivered with the effort not to squirm away, to not use the word. The word. My safeword. During all the years I'd been his "slut slave," I'd never needed to use it. I'd been tempted. And he'd always let me know how much he enjoyed the challenge of pushing me and he often vowed that, before he died, he would break me.

But I'd never used it because I wallowed in everything he did to me. I craved seeing that look of heated pleasure in his eyes.

Sick? Some might say so. But Master M and I made beautiful music together. The counterpoint between sadist and pain slut. The whish of the paddle, my hiss at the blows. His basso-profundo chuckle as my ass turned red, and my moans rising and falling as he forced me to the limits of my endurance. Then that expectant moment—the crescendo when the very air hummed—those times he waited for me to say the word before, with a grunt of satisfied lust, he'd let me have one last, blistering smack. When I punctuated our virtuoso duet with a shrill scream, it was like applause for his rousing performance.

I wrapped this new pain around me as I sank into the memory of our most recent encounter.

He'd been putting me off with excuses of publishing commitments and so I hadn't seen him for several weeks and my body was alive with dark need. I wanted his hands punishing me, anticipated his cruel smile as he watched me accept his commands, and I wanted, no, I hungered for that submissive euphoria that his treatment always evoked.

He had pulled me into his apartment with a rough grasp around my upper arm. Just that brief, pinching twinge set my body thrumming with eager trepidation.

"Take off your clothes, slut." That husky voice in my ear made my cunt throb and drip and I panted with lust for the man and what he was going to do to me. His mood was dark, and while he always loved dirty talk, there was something even more edgy and extreme in his energy that night. He used one hand to grab hold of my hair and yank, and at that moment I sensed he planned to push me beyond any limits we'd heretofore explored. There was just something—an ominous Styxian undercurrent—driving him.

I knew the routine. I pulled my dress over my head and waited. No underwear. Nicely trimmed quim—his term. He got a kick out of the old-fashioned word and it never failed to bring a smile to his face when we were in private and he forced me to lie splayed for him to expound on it, study it, slap it or fuck it.

He flung open his heavy robe and sat down in his chair. His body was big and bearish, strong and fleshy, and his cock fit his frame. I needed no further instructions, because this was our routine.

"A thorough cocksucking to get my motor running," was his favorite cynical turn of phrase, "then the fun really starts."

For me just the sight of him in that chair, his dark eyes glittering, a nasty, evil grin that looked purely devilish on his bearded face, was enough to make my knees weak with the desire to crawl to him. And crawl I did, naked, on my hands and knees, until he could wrap his thick fingers in my hair and pull my face into his groin.

"Come on little slut. Time for Master to fuck your face."

He was not gentle as he shoved into my mouth. Gentleness was not his thing. I might have longed for a soft touch once in a while, but his complete and utter domination of me gave me a sense of protection, of certainty, that was a more than fair trade for me. Lots of men can pat your cheek and whisper sweet nothings, but how many men can make you scream, make you see stars, before they make you come?

Blowing Master M was no easy feat. Not only was he possessed of a hefty cock, but he more or less just wanted a hot wet hole to fuck. It wasn't supposed to be fun for me—it was my slave's duty to make it good for him. I was a receptacle into which he loved spewing. He loved feeling me gag around him, and when all was said and done, if I had snot running down my face and come in my hair he was one happy Master.

A lengthy cocksucking always preceded the pain. It was as if, while he watched himself buried down my throat, he debated which torment he was in the mood to dispense on that occasion. Was he feeling a bit benign and wanted just his handprints covering my butt and thighs before a hearty fucking? Or was he chasing that Mephisthelean mood that sometimes overtook him that meant I was going to be pushed to the limits of my endurance?

That night was one of those nights. I could tell from his

voice, from the extra-rough handling and from the purely filthy monologue that he regaled me with while my mouth was full. He was going to fuck my ass raw. He was going to come on my face, my tits, my cunt. He was in the darkest place I'd ever seen him and when my face was buried against his balls, when I was choking on cock and come, frantic for air before he freed me, I began to quail because I knew what was to come would be a night of volcanic pain.

My hopes (and fears) were confirmed when he tied me down. I hate restraints and bondage and always have. That feeling of absolute helplessness that pushed me into a state of high anxiety and emotion was the one thing I had trouble handling. It frustrated Master M, but he respected my sincere fear. At least, he always had until that night. But I knew that if he demanded to have me at his mercy, he both needed it badly, and was also channeling his inner fiend.

"I'm going to paddle your ass until you use the word."

"I won't use my safeword, Master. I never use the word."

"I'm going to make you use the word. I'm going to break you tonight."

And with that threat he picked up the implement he'd dubbed No Mercy and simply began paddling my ass. It was big, heavy, and it hurt. No warm-up, no massaging, no lewd chitchat about how the mark of the paddle looked good, or how my flesh bounced when he hit me extra hard. Just brutal pain.

He paddled me until I writhed and screamed and begged. He paddled me while I sobbed nonstop, blubbered as my body gave up and I just lay there taking the pain into me, pushing it to the boundary where I tried to turn it into that soul-deep glow. But in the end, he pushed me beyond anything I could take, even for my Master, even though I wanted to let him keep swatting me, exorcising whatever demons drove him.

And maybe the victory over me was what he needed. In the end, I broke.

He had beaten my ass until I used the word.

I'd screamed it.

"Sanctuary!"

And he'd stopped.

Now, as I lay in the tat shop with the needle impaling me like a tiny high-speed drill, I thought about the aftermath of that night. Master M hadn't said a thing when I'd hoarsely croaked out my safeword. He didn't gloat, he didn't rail, he just silently unfastened my wrists and ankles, which ached from wrenching at those bonds.

He said nothing. Just turned and walked out. I lay there trying to wrap my head around what had happened. Why had I let it go on so long? Why had he needed to be so brutal? Had I disappointed him by using the word? He'd seemed determined to drive me to it, so why was he not wallowing in satisfaction at having broken me?

He'd left the room. Left me lying there alone—something he never did. Even as a sadist, he observed the niceties. Making sure I hadn't been pushed someplace emotionally dangerous, that I hadn't suffered more than the tolerable bruises and pain. He wasn't a gentle, lovey-dovey man, but he always stayed with me. He'd sit beside me and talk about his next book, or incongruously, he'd often talk about his children, which, believe me, could be pretty freaking weird while I lay there, naked, with welts all over me.

That night, despite feeling like my entire lower body was on fire, I got scared. I slowly crawled off the bed and held on to the bureau while I got some strength back in my legs. I shuffled stiffly out to the living room of his apartment, past his writing desk and computer. He'd dedicated one of his books to me. *To My Q*, it had read. It amused him that no one would know he'd dedicated it *to my quim*. I continued past the floor-to-ceiling bookcases that held his precious books and photographs. He stood in front of the row of windows that looked out over Central Park.

"Master?" I'd approached him and even gone so far as to touch his arm. Sometimes the transgression earned me a good shaking.

But that night, he pulled me next to him and wrapped one big arm tight around me and just held me.

Gently.

Then he took me to bed and didn't lay a hand on me.

"How are you doing?"

My ink master whispered gently in my ear and I started, suddenly aware that he'd stopped tattooing.

"Mm. I'm fine. No worries."

"All right. Just checking. I've never worked on anyone so relaxed before." He took the soft cloth and wiped it across my ass, then bent back to his work. I envisioned the familiar sight of streaks of my blood on the cloth and smiled. I knew my smile was sad.

The buzzy, bee-stingy heat flared up again, but this time I focused on the pain. Concentrated on the sensation of it seeping through my bloodstream. I desperately wanted that pain. I wanted to feel myself rise as I let it take me, let it sweep me up to the bright place where nothing could reach me.

For the rest of the session I simply experienced it. It wasn't my Master's pain. It was not layered with the domineering raunch of his litany of lewdness. It had none of that tantalizing, itchy tingle of fear engendered by wondering if Master M might go too far. It was not imbued with the glory of submission that made my servitude to him so intense.

It was just a pale echo of Master's hands on my ass.

Then it was over.

My ink master seemed pleased. "I have to say, I had my doubts about the wisdom of this tat, but it is pretty damned cool, if I do say so myself."

"May I have a mirror, please?"

He handed me the hand mirror and I stood up, awkward and a bit stiff, and walked to the full-length mirror. I turned and studied the mark and smiled.

"Mighty fine," I whispered, hearing Master M's growl as I repeated the words I'd heard so often from him as he admired the results of a boisterous ass blistering.

I turned to my artist. "Can you do me a favor? Can you take a picture of the tat and give me a printout?"

If he thought the request was a weird one, he didn't say so or shrug. He just nodded, picked up a digital camera and took two shots of my ass. He printed them both out; one was perfect. Exactly what I wanted to give to my Master. I folded it neatly and put it in an envelope. The other one I folded and shoved into my bag.

My mind had already left the building when I paid the balance for my tat, thanked the ink master and walked out of the shop. I was late so I walked as quickly as my sore ass would allow and jumped on the C train. A lovely young Hispanic gentleman offered me his seat, but I simply declined and smiled. I wouldn't be sitting for a while. That was the other reason I'd taken the next week off. I knew I'd need time to heal. Just as I'd known after that last night that something had changed. Something that would alter my life. Master M never spoke to me about that night. About my refuge in sanctuary. About his rare gentle embrace that would haunt me always. He never revealed where the darkness had come from. But I was afraid I knew. In the end I knew my Master too well not to know.

I was late, but I slipped into the building near Master M's apartment and stood in the back of the room. Apparently the event had concluded, which was actually preferable as far as I was concerned. I needed a final moment of private communion, so I waited quietly as the remaining visitors exited and then I walked slowly up to the front of the room.

I pulled out the envelope with the image of my tattoo. I took the picture out and stared down at it. Then I placed the photo beneath my Master's hands.

He'd often made me cry. Physical pain could do that to a person. It had only meant that we'd had a good time in our own perverted way. Consummate sadist that he was, he'd loved me hard and without reservation. And I loved him. He was my heart. I'd feel the beat of him inside me, always. The beat of his presence in my life. The memories of his possessive hands on my flesh. The satisfaction that I'd belonged to him, body and soul.

I looked down for the last time at my Master's hands. The big knuckles and the thick fingers. I couldn't help but smile. One broad palm rested across the picture of my ass. Across the tattoo of his handprint in blazing red across my right cheek.

The room was utterly silent. I leaned in close and whispered, "I hope you've found your sanctuary, Master." I touched those hands one last time. Then I turned and left.

I didn't answer the one man who stood waiting outside the door. I couldn't speak. Just nodded as he gave me his regrets.

I walked slowly and felt the burning in my ass like a throbbing wound, paling beside the hollow wrenching agony in my chest. I knew the pain in my flesh would dull. Fade. But for now it fueled the other pain. The pain that cut right to my heart. A pain I could not bear.

But there was no safeword to stop this pain.

I stopped and pulled out the second copy of my tattoo. I unfolded it and looked down at the brilliantly rendered image. Perfectly lifelike. Almost as if I'd just been smacked on the ass by a big, broad hand.

Unlike the memories of pain, it would never fade. It would always be there like a comforting caress.

My Master's mark.

ABOUT THE AUTHORS

LISETTE ASHTON is the author of more than two dozen erotic novels, including *Beyond Temptation* and *Dragon Desire*. When not writing novels, Lisette writes short stories, with work published in a variety of anthologies including *The Mammoth Book of Best New Erotica, Open for Business* and *The Sweetest Kiss*.

VICTORIA BEHN is a prize-winning poet and storyteller based in the northwest of England. She is currently working in her community offering workshops and promoting creative writing. Her oral storytelling performance won the Spoken Word Award at the Buxton Fringe in 2012.

ERZABET BISHOP (erzabetsenchantments.blogspot.com) has been writing since she could punch keys on a typewriter. She is the author of *Erotic Wiccans: Beltane Fires*, "Dark Hunger" in the *Coming Together Hungry for Love* anthology and a contributing author in *Milk & Cookies & Handcuffs*.

RACHEL KRAMER BUSSEL (rachelkramerbussel.com) is the editor of *Please, Sir; Yes, Sir; He's on Top; Cheeky Spanking Stories; Spanked; Bottoms Up; Anything for You: Erotica for Kinky Couples; Twice the Pleasure; Bisexual Women's Erotica; Baby Got Back: Anal Erotica; Best Bondage Erotica 2011, 2012, 2013* and many other erotica anthologies.

ROSE CARAWAY hails from Sacramento, California. She is a writer, narrator, producer and podcaster for the hit show, *The Kiss Me Quick's* erotica podcast, and she is constantly seeking the best stories in erotica—for her own personal pleasure as well as sharing a few with her faithful Lurid Listeners.

DEBORAH CASTELLANO (deborahmcastellano.com) has appeared in a number of erotica anthologies including *Dead Sexy, Best Lesbian Erotica 2012, Anything for You* and *Best Women's Erotica 2009*. She recently made her nonfiction debut with *The Arte of Glamour*.

CECILIA DUVALLE (ceciliaduvalle.com) is a writer, blogger, knitter and mother. Her work is available in anthologies via Cleis Press, Ravenous Romance and Xcite Books. She writes about sex and writing sexy stuff on her blog, and she enjoys steamy electronic role-play. She lives in suburbia near Seattle.

NINA FAIRWEATHER is a previously unpublished reverse superhero. She leaps server racks with a single ladder by day and is a mild-mannered wordsmith by night. She adores the ghosts of old buildings, navigates the streets of Seattle by bicycle, and has yet to find a submissive who can sew.

GRAYDANCER's (graydancer.com) sex-positive fiction and nonfiction has appeared in many anthologies. He is a sex educator, performer and activist and part of the Erotication websites. He is known for his Ropecast (a kinky podcast) and kinky unconferences (GRUEs) throughout the world.

LYDIA HILL is the erotica pseudonym of author Lise Horton. Her erotic romance novel from Carina Press debuts in Fall 2013. She always strives to entertain, whether writing intense erotic fiction or romance. She dedicates this story, and all her fiction, to the memory of Milton.

SOMMER MARSDEN (sommermarsden.blogspot.com) has been called "...one of the top storytellers in the erotica genre" (Violet Blue), and "Unapologetic" (Alison Tyler). Her erotic novels include *Boys Next Door*, *Learning to Drown* and *Restless Spirit*.

EVAN MORA's stories of kinky pleasure have appeared in numerous anthologies, including *Best Bondage Erotica 2011* and *2013*, *Cheeky Spanking Stories* and *Under Her Thumb*. She lives in Toronto.

NYM NIX is an Australian writer living in Canberra. She lives at the foot of a mountain, in an old house, and kangaroos occasionally visit her front garden. Her imagination, on the other hand, lives anywhere but in reality. She also occasionally publishes speculative fiction under another name.

GISELLE RENARDE is a queer Canadian, avid volunteer, contributor to more than one hundred short-story anthologies and author of numerous electronic and print books, including

Anonymous, *Nanny State* and *My Mistress' Thighs*. Ms. Renarde lives across from a park with two bilingual cats who sleep on her head.

TERESA NOELLE ROBERTS (teresanoelleroberts.com) writes sexy stories for lusty romantics. Look for BDSM romance *Knowing the Ropes* and the erotic paranormal *Duals and Donovans* series (newest: *Cougar's Courage)* from Samhain. Her work appears in *Best Bondage Erotica 2011, 2012* and *2013,* and in other provocatively titled anthologies.

THOMAS S. ROCHE's (thomasroche.com) stories have appeared in more than four hundred publications. His zombie novel *The Panama Laugh* was a finalist for the Horror Writers' Association's Bram Stoker Award, and his story "Butterfly's Kiss" was a finalist for the National Leather Association's John Preston Award.

LISABET SARAI (lisabetsarai.com) occasionally tackles other genres, but BDSM will always be her first love. Every one of her eight novels includes some element of power exchange, while her D/s short-story collections *Just a Spanking* and *Spank Me Again, Stranger* range from mildly kinky to intensely perverse.

DONNA GEORGE STOREY (DonnaGeorgeStorey.com) is the author of *Amorous Woman,* an erotic novel based on her own experiences living in Japan. Her adults-only tales have appeared in numerous places including *Penthouse, The Mammoth Book of Erotica Presents the Best of Donna George Storey, Best Women's Erotica, Best Erotic Romance* and *The Big Book of Bondage.*

ALISON TYLER (alisontyler.blogspot.com), the "Trollop with a Laptop," has written twenty-five erotic novels and edited more than sixty erotic anthologies including *Twisted*, *Torn* and *Smart Ass*. In all things important, she remains faithful to her partner of seventeen years, but she still can't choose just one perfume.

VERONICA WILDE (veronicawilde.com) is an erotic romance author whose work has been published by Cleis Press, Bella Books, Liquid Silver Books, Samhain Publishing and Xcite Books.

CELA WINTER took up writing after a career as a restaurant chef. She has published erotic fiction in print and on the web. A resident of the Pacific Northwest, she is working on a novel, when the Muse isn't distracting her with short-story ideas.

ABOUT
THE EDITOR

D. L. KING (dlkingerotica.com) spends an inordinate amount of time reading and writing smut in her New York City apartment and postage stamp-sized garden. She is the editor of *Under Her Thumb: Erotic Stories of Female Domination, Seductress: Erotic Tales of Immortal Desire, The Harder She Comes: Butch/Femme Erotica,* (winner of the Lambda Literary Award and Independent Publisher Book Award Gold Medal), *Carnal Machines: Steampunk Erotica* (also a gold medalist), *The Sweetest Kiss: Ravishing Vampire Erotica* and the Lambda Literary Award Finalist, *Where the Girls Are: Urban Lesbian Erotica.* D. L. King is the publisher and editor of the erotica review site, Erotica Revealed. She is the author of dozens of short stories, and her work can be found in various editions of *Best Lesbian Erotica, Best Women's Erotica, Best Bondage Erotica, The Mammoth Book of Best New Erotica,* as well as many other titles such as *The Big Book of Bondage; Anything for You; One Night Only; Power Play; Lucious; Hurts So Good;*

Fast Girls; *Gotta Have It*; *Please, Ma'am*; *Yes, Sir*; *Frenzy* and more. She is the author of two novels of female domination and male submission, *The Melinoe Project* and *The Art of Melinoe*.

More from D. L. King

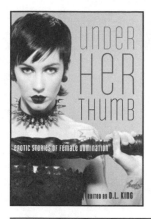

Under Her Thumb
Erotic Stories of Female Domination
Edited by D. L. King

Under Her Thumb will whet your appetite for all things femdom. These fierce tops know how to dominate their men—and the occasional woman. Award-winning editor D. L. King serves up a feast to be savored by tops, bottoms and the wonderfully curious.
ISBN 978-1-57344-927-4 $15.95

Seductress
Erotic Tales of Immortal Desire
Edited by D. L. King

A succubus is a sexual vampire, a shape-shifting temptress who steals the life force from her victim—but what a way to go! Award-winning editor D. L. King has crafted a singularly sexy and mysterious compilation that will have you lying in bed all night wondering who might visit.
ISBN 978-1-57344-819-2 $15.95

The Harder She Comes
Butch/Femme Erotica
Edited by D. L. King

Some butches worship at the altar of their femmes, and many adorable girls long for the embrace of their suave, sexy daddies. In *The Harder She Comes*, we meet femmes who salivate at the sight of packed jeans and bois who dream of touching the corseted waist of a beautiful, confident woman.
ISBN 978-1-57344-778-2 $14.95

Carnal Machines
Steampunk Erotica
Edited by D. L. King

D. L. King has curated stories by outstanding contemporary erotica writers who use the enthralling possibilities of the 19th-century steam age to tease and titillate in a decadent fusing of technology and romance.
ISBN 978-1-57344-654-9 $14.95

The Sweetest Kiss
Ravishing Vampire Erotica
Edited by D. L. King

These blood-drenched tales give new meaning to the term "dead sexy" and feature beautiful bloodsuckers whose desires go far beyond blood. Enter these shadowy alleys and dark bedrooms to experience the frisson of terror and delight that only a vampire can inspire.
978-1-57344-371-5 $15.95

Ordering is easy! Call us toll free or fax us to place your MC/VISA order.
You can also mail the order form below with payment to:
Cleis Press, 2246 Sixth St., Berkeley, CA 94710.

ORDER FORM

QTY	TITLE	PRICE
___	_____	_____
___	_____	_____
___	_____	_____
___	_____	_____
___	_____	_____
___	_____	_____
___	_____	_____
___	_____	_____

SUBTOTAL   _____

SHIPPING   _____

SALES TAX   _____

TOTAL   _____

Add $3.95 postage/handling for the first book ordered and $1.00 for each additional book. Outside North America, please contact us for shipping rates. California residents add 9% sales tax. Payment in U.S. dollars only.

* Free book of equal or lesser value. Shipping and applicable sales tax extra.

Cleis Press • Phone: (800) 780-2279 • Fax: (510) 845-8001
orders@cleispress.com • www.cleispress.com
You'll find more great books on our website

Follow us on Twitter @cleispress • Friend/fan us on Facebook